The Russian Library

General Editor
ROBERT PAYNE

TITLES IN PRINT

SISTER MY LIFE
by Boris Pasternak. *Translated by*
Phillip C. Flayderman.

THE ISLAND: A JOURNEY TO SAKHALIN
by Anton Chekhov. *Translated by Luba and*
Michael Terpak.

THE TALE OF THE UNEXTINGUISHED
MOON AND OTHER STORIES
by Boris Pilnyak. *Translated by Beatrice Scott.*

LOVE AND OTHER STORIES
by Yuri Olyesha. *Translated by Robert Payne.*

THE COMPLETE PLAYS OF
VLADIMIR MAYAKOVSKY
Translated by Guy Daniels.

THE SUNNY NIGHT
by Nodar Dumbadze. *Translated by*
George Nakashidse.

IN PREPARATION

SELECTED POEMS OF ANNA AKHMATOVA
Translated by Carole W. Bartlett.

CORRESPONDENCE WITH FRIENDS
by Nikolai Gogol. *Translated by Arthur Hudgins.*

SELECTED POEMS OF OSIP MANDELSHTAM
Translated by Peter Russell.

THE APOCALYPSE OF OUR TIME
by V. V. Rozanov. *Translated by Janet Romanoff.*

AN ANTHOLOGY OF GEORGIAN POETRY
Translated by George Nakashidse.

BLOCKADE
by Anatol Daroff. *Translated by Rosalind A. Zoglin.*

AN ANTHOLOGY OF RUSSIAN POETRY
Translated by Guy Daniels.

NOTEBOOK OF A PHYSICIAN AND
OTHER STORIES
by Michael Bulgakov. *Translated by Michael Glenny.*

THE SUNNY NIGHT

THE
SUNNY
NIGHT

—

Nodar Dumbadze

Translated by
George Nakashidse

With an Introduction by
Robert Payne

WASHINGTON SQUARE PRESS, INC. • NEW YORK

The translator would like to
acknowledge the kindly assistance
given to him by Patricia Mindlin.

Contents

Introduction

Somewhere about the middle of the nineteenth century there occurred a strange change in the nature of the novel. Where previously the novelist was concerned with the human animal in all his dimensions, now quite suddenly the human envelope was stripped away and the novel became increasingly concerned with the adventures of the soul. In *War and Peace* Pierre Bezukhov and Prince Andrey Bolkonsky are almost disembodied presences, and though we might recognize them if they entered the room, we know the inner workings of their minds and the delicate movements of their souls even more intimately than we know their physical appearance. By the time Dostoyevsky came to write his major novels, the physical presence of the characters vanishes altogether and we are left with fierce tensions and fields of force working in an atmosphere of brooding violence. What interested Dostoyevsky was not the adventures of people so much as the wanderings and expectations of their souls. The soul, divested of human ornaments, was seen to be a landscape of almost unimaginable proportions, and always a battleground.

The map of the human soul, as the novelists charted it, was far more complex than anyone had suspected. There were no compass bearings; the contradictions were everywhere, and nothing was what it seemed to be. The sunlight blazed in the darkness of night, the dead lived, the innocent were guilty and the specter you saw in the forest a moment ago was yourself returning from an errand of mercy. At the crossroads there was one's own heart with a stake driven through it, but the heart was still beating. The landscape of the soul was as strange as an African mask, and far less easy to understand.

This attitude toward the human soul found its expression in all the European languages. The soul was breaking up and assuming strange forms in all the countries of the West, and a new kind of sensibility was needed to come to terms with it. Even in remote Georgia, conquered by the Tsars but still retaining its own language and a fierce spirit of independence, the new techniques were being studied, and a new literature was being born.

The Georgians suffer from having a language that few Westerners have ever learned. It is a remarkably subtle and fluid language, and the Georgian novelists of the nineteenth century were quick to make their own discoveries in the landscape of the soul. A whole galaxy of novelists, their names little known in the West, arose to grapple with the new themes. Georgian literature, which had achieved memorable heights in the reign of Queen Thamar in the Middle Ages, once again blazed furiously into life. A tradition was established: to a medieval romanticism they added the quick perception of the most subtle movements of the human character. Under the Soviets they have continued to write in their own language, with their own characteristic delight in the intricate mechanism of the soul. They see the world by the light of the flashing snows of the Caucasus Mountains.

Nodar Dumbadze belongs to the nineteenth-century tradition, even though he has a peculiarly modern sensibility. What interests him are the movements of the soul, God, love, the fragility of life, the imminence of death. He wants to know what the soul is doing and where it is going, and whether there is any hope for it. He accepts the existence of miracles, because, as he observes, they happen to him every day. His hero, Teymuraz Baramidze, is a young student earnestly attempting to confront his own soul and see himself as he is. As for miracles, he has received the greatest miracle of all, for his mother has been given back to him after being imprisoned for twelve years in Stalin's concentration camps. No one asks her what she suffered in the concentration camp, or why her husband did not return with her. It is enough that she has returned from the dead and lives once more in her old apartment. When she was arrested he was still a boy; now that he is a man he sees her with a tormenting tenderness. She is the bread and the wine, the resurrection of the flesh.

There is a sense in which the mother returned from the dead is the chief character of the story. She makes no demands on her son, and she is never described at any length, but her shadow falls over the story like the shadow of an ancient oak tree which has been struck by lightning but still throws out its green leaves; and the other characters play in her shade.

When Nodar Dumbadze writes about the mother, we are aware of a new note in Soviet literature—a note of intense religious feeling expressed without any reserve, with gaiety and intelligence. It is not the voice of the Russian Orthodox Church, but of some earlier, long-forgotten, more primitive church confronted with real and pressing problems which cannot wait for a solution. These young students talk all night, like students everywhere, about the nature of the world and of God,

and they come to solutions which would surprise their
Communist masters. Here is Guram, the close friend of
the narrator, discussing the mother who has returned
from the concentration camp:

"Do you know who your mother is?" Guram asked me.

I had no answer. Guram looked at me for a long time,
a very long time, then poured some wine in his glass
and began:

"Your mother is God. That you sit and look at her, and
she sits and looks at you, that you call her Mother
and she calls you son. Do you think there is no God?
Who do you think God is? A bearded grandfather who
sits on a cloud and washes His face and makes the rain?
God is so clear, so near, so obvious and so simple that
when you see Him, you don't know that He is God, you
cannot imagine that He is God, you cannot believe that
He is God. That is God's misfortune. That's why people
have no faith in God. If God were somewhere else, far
from us, alone and on high, if God were not among us,
then everyone would believe in Him! That is the absolute
truth! You must believe in God even though He has no
face. When He is there, when He does not say He is God,
when He breaks bread with you, prepares your dinner,
dresses you, covers your head, smiles at you and caresses
you, kisses you, weeps because of you, is cold, thirsty
and hungry with you, dies for you, gives His soul to the
devil for your sake—then you must believe in such a
God. But when God shows you His face, stands you in
the corner, pulls your ears, and says to you: 'I am God,
believe in Me,' then why does He need your faith?
Not only you, but everyone will accept such a God.
You must believe in God when He is like you, like me,
like your mother. Do you understand?"

Guram speaks about God with a casual familiarity
which is breathtaking. He has no interest at all in
theological problems. What interests him above all is
surviving under a Communist dictatorship while retaining some shreds of human dignity, and enjoying the

company of his friends. He is very down to earth, warm-hearted and intelligent, in spite of the fact that he makes poor grades at the university. There is more than the suspicion that a man who makes good grades at the university must be something of a monster.

Although Nodar Dumbadze is a Georgian describing a peculiarly Georgian scene—for the novel is set in Tiflis with a brief excursion to Batum—his young students are like young students everywhere else in the world. Essentially this is a novel about students attempting to discover themselves, sometimes succeeding in the attempt, but more often failing ludicrously because the scales are so heavily weighted against them. They have to contend with the usual flinty-eyed rectors and leaden-hearted examiners, and in addition there are the political party hacks who are designed by God to act out the role of the ten plagues of Egypt. Dumbadze evidently knows them well and caricatures them unmercifully. The narrator's attitude toward the regimentation in the university appears to have been one of unrelieved disenchantment, although he is enchanted with everyone he meets. In much the same way an American writer might write about an American university, for almost by definition a university is a place of disenchantment.

Nodar Dumbadze has, however, one advantage over the writer in the West. He has the characteristically Georgian temperament, at once genuinely lyrical and earthy, sensuous and sensual, romantic and classical. He has the gift of bringing his characters to life in a few brief, sure strokes. He describes the arrest of the mother in a single sentence: ". . . she had been taken away by two men; one of them seemed to be afraid, while the other smiled, showing a mouth full of silver teeth." In this way he suggests the dark era of Stalinist repression, and it is enough. He has said exactly what has to be said in the most classical way. Not that he is incapable of romantic frenzies, for when the narrator describes his beloved Tiflis at night, or his first sexual

experience, or an idiotic play about the death of Hitler
staged by some eighth-grade students, he will simply follow his instincts and abandon all classical restraints.
Romanticism is apt to run its full course in any novel
written by a Georgian.

The girl student Gulika describes the narrator as
"the most sympathetic of all the sympathetic fools!
Never in the history of mankind has there been such a
red-gold fool like him." But this is only her way of
describing his remarkable sanity. She is half in love
with him, and she understands him only too well. She
will inevitably lose him to the plump Lida and the
earthy Lia, whose appearance in a cherry-red bathing
suit is not calculated to make his life more comfortable.
Lida lost her husband in the war and found solace in
religion. Lia will never lose her husband and never find
solace except in her own beautiful and earthbound
body. The narrator knows that he will always be at the
mercy of the women who enter his life. The battle lines
are clearly drawn, and he fights with whatever weapons
are available.

Then there is Uncle Abibo, and he must be fought
with sterner weapons, for he is the living representative
of the treachery at the heart of Stalinist society. When
Thavera, another young student, escapes from prison,
Teymuraz Baramidze must defend him as best he can.
He has a deep affection for Thavera, and knows that
terrible punishments are given to escaped prisoners. In
utter despair he approaches Uncle Abibo, who has con-
nections with the secret police, and he must have
known from the beginning that one does not put one's
trust in the secret police. Uncle Abibo, with his marble-
top table and deer antlers hung with swords, is a figure
out of a *danse macabre*, but he, too, is perfectly realized.
He does exactly what is expected of him: he throws
Thavera to the wolves. When at last Uncle Abibo lies
dying, Teymuraz Baramidze realizes that death is about
to claim something which has always been deathly and
obscene; and even for such deaths one must grieve.

When the mother dies so shortly after being released from prison, then there is another kind of grief altogether, because death is claiming someone who was beautiful and vividly alive. The story of her death is told quietly and solemnly, as though to music. A few weeks later he is standing beside her grave:

> I have come. It is I, your flesh and blood, standing beside your tombstone. . . . I am your child. . . . I stand here among the graves at midnight and I am not afraid. I am not afraid because the thing I feared above all has already happened. That was your death; and because I no longer fear death, I no longer fear life.
>
> It does not disturb me that this cemetery like many others is being turned into a park, a large and pretty park. I have planted a lime tree on your grave. I will make it grow and blossom. In the future, Lia and I will come to your grave with our children, and the tree will have grown into a vast, green, cool shade, and my children will play in your greenness, your coolness and shade. Perhaps they will carve their names on your breast, but don't be hurt: the same thing will probably happen at my grave and Lia's grave. The lime tree will blossom and grow and every one of our graves will become part of the life of this world. And every cemetery will be turned into a park, and so it will be for all eternity.

In such passages as these Nodar Dumbadze shows that he descends in the great tradition of the nineteenth-century novelists.

II

This is the first of Nodar Dumbadze's works to appear in English. *The Sunny Night* was first published in the literary magazine *Mnathobi* (*The Lightbringer*) in January and February 1966. The literary magazine is edited by Gregor Abashidze, one of the leading Georgian poets and novelists. Like *Novy Mir*, the Georgian journal is noted for its liberalism.

Nodar Dumbadze has written two other novels—*I See the Sun*, and *I, Iliko, Ilarion and the Grandmother*. Both of them were made into films. He has written poetry and film scenarios. *The Sunny Night* appears to be largely autobiographical. No other information about him is available.

It scarcely matters that we know so little about him, for he has revealed himself abundantly in *The Sunny Night*. He has held nothing back. He shows us the lives of the students of Tiflis as they are, and for the first time we are permitted to come face to face with students in a university in the Soviet Union. It is a tribute to his artistic skill that we never find ourselves doubting his story, which he tells with so much generosity and sympathy.

Robert Payne

THE SUNNY NIGHT

A Birthday

There was weeping and gnashing of teeth in room 107. The distinguished Professor Kassiane Gogichaishvili was supervising the political economy examinations. This was not unusual, and none of us was the least worried, until Liuba Nodia came out, tears running down her cheeks, and told us that he had been able to hear everything. All of a sudden we were dry as a bone.

Who would have guessed that this kind deaf man to whom it was possible to say anything at all—instead of describing the mercantile system, you could as well talk about clover roots, and still get an "A"—would recover his hearing during the spring examinations?

11

When I heard the news, I knew that as far as I was concerned the result of the examination was settled. However, my curiosity got the better of me, and I ran up to Liuba, who looked like an overripe yellow melon. She was staring down at the "D" marked in her matriculation certificate.

"What's the matter?" I asked her, pulling at her sleeve.

"What am I supposed to do with this?" she answered, peering at me expressionlessly.

"Doesn't the fool know that a "D" cannot be entered in a matriculation certificate?" Guram asked.

"I *told* him, but he just said, 'How should I know, my girl? This is the first time in my life I've given anyone a "D." ' What am I supposed to do with this?" Liuba said, and her eyes filled with tears.

"What questions did you draw?" Guram asked.

"The first was about the distribution of goods, and the second was about inflation. I can't remember the third."

"Couldn't you answer anything?"

"I started—"

"What did you say?"

"The same thing as last year—that I was in the country during the summer helping my grandmother in the orchard . . . and my grandmother is a very good-humored woman—you know how it is—

" 'If that's the case,' he said, 'then your grandmother can give you a good grade,' " Liuba said, and fell silent. She burst into tears over her matriculation certificate.

The door to the lecture room opened and the proctor, reading from a list, announced: "Baramidze and Tchitchinadze may come in."

"Since when does T come immediately after B, idiot?" Guram said.

"One off the top of the list and one from the bottom," the proctor explained. He looked in the direction of the lecture room as if to say: "It's not my fault—the professor gave the orders."

I don't know the name of the disease: your heart comes up into your throat, your tongue descends to your stomach, cold sweat pours off your forehead, your knees are numb, your hands tremble and your eyes grow dim. When I looked at Guram and saw him wiping his forehead and hands with a large handkerchief and then flicking his tongue over his dry lips, I knew it was contagious.

We went in on tiptoe. The professor was sitting behind a table covered in green felt, smiling. He wore gold-rimmed spectacles with thick lenses, and each earpiece was fitted out with a hearing-aid—the instrument of our destruction.

"Sit down, please," he said. We did not move.

"Have you gone deaf? Please come and sit down," he repeated.

We sat down at the table on which, like death sentences, the small, white and still virginal examination papers were lying.

"Take a paper and think over your reply," the professor said.

I picked up a paper, turned it over, and knew at once that I could think over these questions until the day of my death, but I would never find the answers.

Guram also chose one, looked at it and stared at me like a bull-calf being led to the slaughter.

"What is your first and last name?" the professor asked.

"Teymuraz Baramidze," I replied.

The professor wrote my answer down in a notebook.

"And yours?" he asked, turning to Guram.

"Guram Tchitchinadze," he replied, as bravely as I had.

The professor took that down too.

Guram and I were sitting at some distance from

one another, as required by the examination rules. I began to read my paper, strangely indifferent. The first question was on land rent. "Will you begin?" the professor asked me, suddenly.

"Why not?" I replied. Guram's mouth fell open in surprise.

"Do so, then," the professor answered, seemingly delighted with my reply.

"Land rent: land is sold in capitalistic countries. Everything is sold there, in general, including conscience—and it would seem that this is sold quite cheaply. Rent is a tax on land. Taxes in the capitalistic world are very high and the peasants suffer under the yoke of military expenditure because of capitalistic saber-rattling. Armament demands enormous expenditure. For enormous expenditures enormous amounts of money must be found. Where does it come from? The logic of experience tells us. From land taxation, naturally!"

"What do they call you, young man?" the professor interrupted me.

"Teymo, sir."

"Did you attend my lectures?"

"Can you doubt it, sir?" I replied, with the air of someone hurt by his question.

"I'm not sure I remember you. And I certainly don't know *you*," he said, turning to Guram.

"But we know you, sir. You are Kassiane Gogichaishvili, our favorite professor, our pride! Who would think of missing your lectures? We not only take notes on them, we devour them!" Guram was transported by enthusiasm.

"Describe then, if you please, what you have devoured," the professor said, cutting him short.

Guram seemed suddenly turned to stone: then, like a dog coming out of the water, he shook his head and looked over at me. I bit my tongue to prevent myself from laughing out loud. Then he turned to the professor.

"Well, if you please," the professor said, urging him.

"Have you finished with Baramidze, sir?" Guram asked in a feeble voice, favoring me with a smile full of generosity.

"Baramidze can be thinking over the other question," the professor said.

Guram glanced down once more at his paper and then looked up at the ceiling, and he began to read something which seemed to be written there, or perhaps it was in his brain. Then it appeared that whatever he had been reading went blank, and he came back to earth.

"Would it possibly be . . . Is it possible, sir, to pick another subject?" Guram asked suddenly.

"It is possible," the professor answered, heaving a sigh.

Guram's trembling fingers hovered above the sheets of papers and then paused for a long instant. "Tchitchinadze, there are other students to be examined besides yourself," the professor said.

Guram's hand moved mechanically and another paper seemed to attach itself to it. He held it up to his eyes and his lips moved, as if he were reciting the words himself.

"Well then! What do you say?" asked the professor, drumming his fingers nervously on the table.

"How many times is it possible to choose another subject, sir?" Guram asked. His voice cracked.

"Give me your matriculation certificate," the professor said, stretching out his hand.

Guram's courage deserted him. "Don't fail me, sir," he cried. "I'll lose my scholarship!"

"Who cares about your scholarship! I lost a friend whom I hadn't seen for twenty years, but that didn't kill me."

"It would seem that he had already been lost to you for a long time. And what happened to this poor man?" Guram asked, as though his heart were melting.

"Tchitchinadze, give me your matriculation certificate," the professor said.

"Help me," Guram's eyes pleaded with me.

"Sir, honored sir, it would be a great injustice were you to give him a 'D,'" I said, putting in a word for Guram. "We've been up studying together all night."

"My dear young man, at Oxford I studied with Chamberlain—not only for one night, but for five whole years. He later became Prime Minister of England. Here I am in Tiflis teaching idiots such as yourselves. Do I make myself clear?"

Clear as day. But Guram was unwilling to retreat. "Sir, Professor, imagine that you were a millionaire, and that you had millions of 'C's' at your disposal. A beggar comes to you and says, 'O honorable millionaire, do me a little favor, if it is possible, give me one little "C."' Imagine, imagine that I am this beggar, and that I am asking you ..."

I was unable to stand more of this dialogue between the millionaire and the wretched beggar. Covering my face with my hands, I ran out. There was no one in the corridor, and so there was no one to ask me what grade I received.

Only Gulika wordlessly followed me down to the end of the hall. When I did not look at her, she turned away. I went down the stairs, but on the last step I felt her looking down at me, and turned to look back. She stood at the head of the stairs with her chin resting on her hands and elbows on the balustrade. She did not take her eyes off me.

"What are you looking at?" I asked.

Gulika straightened up, shook her head and walked away.

I went out into the university garden and sat down on a bench. In front of me, a little girl was digging in the ground with a spade, throwing the dirt at the feet of a little boy who smiled and stood obediently before her, like a young tree freshly planted. The

girl looked up at him from time to time, to see if
he had begun to grow, and then dug up some more
dirt and threw it on his feet. The little boy stood
there obedient and motionless, and—probably because he was expecting to grow—he was smiling con-
tinually.

It was a warm green May day in the garden. Now,
on this very day, my government's stipend—thanks to
my "D"—was reduced by 275 rubles 40 kopeks. A
scholarship seems to consist of miraculous money
falling from the sky. As an honest man, I had always
wondered about three things. First, why did they give
me a scholarship? Second, why did they put a tax on
it? Third, why did I have to pay tuition? Despite all
this, I could not think of anyone in the world who
needed a scholarship more than I did, or who appre-
ciated it more. And what now? I sat in the garden of
the university, without a scholarship, watching this
funny little girl who had by now finished planting
the little boy and had begun to water him.

The boy who had been planted looked up and
grinned at me.

"What's your name?" I asked.

"His name is Lasho, and mine is Ia," the little girl
said, answering for both of them.

"Aren't you afraid he'll catch cold if you pour water
on his feet?"

"He has to grow!"

"Nobody grows like that. Look at me. When I was
your size I ate a lot, and see how big I am now."

I thought of my childhood. The little girl looked
at me dubiously.

"What did you eat?" she asked suddenly.

"Bread and butter, milk, porridge, cakes," I began,
counting on my fingers. I had begun with the little
finger, and when I reached my thumb, I swallowed
my saliva and stopped.

"And now?" asked the little girl.

"Now what?" I said.

"Now what do you eat?"

"Now? This and that . . . but I have no idea what I will eat in the future—that is something I don't know."

I smiled at the little girl.

"Why?" she asked.

"Why? Because I just lost a scholarship."

"What?"

"A scholarship."

"Where did you lose it?"

"Where did I lose what?"

"That whatever-you-said?"

God, how children ask questions!

"I didn't lose anything. I was only joking."

"Tell me. What have you lost?"

"Perpetual motion."

"What?"

"Per-pet-u-al mo-tion," I said, carefully, happy that she was unable to pronounce this word and would finally leave me in peace. However, a miracle happened.

"Perpedutomotion?" said the little boy.

"Hello! So you have grown already! Well, that's enough. Now you can get out of the mud."

I tried to change the subject.

"Don't move, don't move! If you do, you'll crumble!" Ia warned him.

The little boy remained planted.

"Are you strong?" Lasho asked me.

"Pretty strong."

"Show me your muscles."

I bent my arm and flexed my biceps. The little boy pressed my arm with his index finger and then hiccoughed, as though to indicate his approval. He said: "Are you stronger than a mountain?"

"Of course."

"Than a bear?"

"Yes!"

I made a face.

"Can you beat Uncle Stalin?" the boy said suddenly, and waited, holding his breath.

I looked around me. The little girl was motionless, waiting to hear what I would say. I said nothing.

"Can you beat Uncle Stalin?" she said.

"Nobody can beat him, my dear," I answered and stood up. The children sighed with relief.

"That's enough. You've already grown!" I exclaimed, putting my hands on Lasho's shoulders and lifting him a little. I dug him out of the ground. He moved his feet cheerfully, knocking one against the other to shake off the mud.

"Good-bye! When you get home, eat some bread and butter before going to bed, and in the morning you will wake up a big man," I said, kissing the boy and putting him down.

"Are you leaving?" Lasho said, heartbroken.

"I'm going. Show me your muscles."

Lasho bent his thin arm, strained the veins of his neck, held his breath and peered up at me. I pressed my finger on his biceps.

"Well, well," I exclaimed, as though surprised. "How strong you are!"

Lasho's face brightened and he looked at Ia.

"Tomorrow I'll be even stronger, because I'll eat bread and butter!" he said.

"Then be a brave boy and keep your promise, if you want to be my friend," I said, and left the garden.

I have a room on the fourth floor of a house on the right side of the Varasi ravine. I have good neighbors on the east and west; on the north I have a view of a rubbish heap and on the south I look out on the university. My room is twenty-six meters square, but in the housing office it is twenty, so that it can be rented at a special low price. My room has two beds, one desk, three chairs and a cupboard. The cupboard contains three and one-half plates, four cups, four spoons and forks. I am the hanger for my clothes, since all I own are on my back. For this reason, when I go out, I either leave the key with the first neighbor I happen to meet or simply leave my door unlocked.

I went up the stairs reluctantly. The hall door was open. I half opened the door to my room and stopped, petrified. A shudder ran through my entire body and my knees trembled. The room was full of my neighbors. They surrounded the bed, on which a thin, pale-faced woman—middle-aged, gray, terribly tired—was sitting. She smiled and said something in a weak, low voice. Nobody paid any attention to me. The gray woman looked at me quietly and briefly and then went on with her story. The neighbors shook their heads, as though they were suffering from guilt.

The gray woman suddenly stopped and stared intently at me for a long time. Then she looked back at the neighbors, who turned to the door. A silence like death fell over the room. I heard nothing but the beating of my heart and the creaking of a chair. The gray woman did not take her eyes off me. Suddenly frightened, she turned to my next-door neighbor, Eliko.

Eliko nodded, as though in agreement. The gray woman got up, her hands and lips trembling. She resembled in a strange way that same woman who, twelve years ago, in this very room, had awakened me at four o'clock in the morning, blessed me and kissed me. Then she had been taken away by two men; one of them seemed to be afraid, while the other smiled, showing a mouth full of silver teeth.

This was my mother. Now, only three steps separated us. She walked slowly—very slowly—toward me. I could hear her breathing. I wanted to turn and run, but I could not. I simply closed my eyes and waited. Then I felt her head on my shoulder and I heard her whisper very softly: "How are you, my son?"

"How are you, my son?" she repeated, over and over, for a long time, a very long time. "How are you, my son?" I knew she was waiting for me to say: "How are you, Mother?" but I could not.

"How are you, ma'am?" I said, and began to cry.

I sit in the kitchen and look at the row of plane trees in front of the university. One, two, three, four . . . Probably the neighbors have gone to bed. Eliko will not come to say, "Go to your room, boy. Are you a stone? Have some pity on the poor woman . . ." . . . five, six . . . Probably she has gone to bed, too. She asked me nothing: nothing about the course I am taking, what faculty I am studying in, how I am . . . seven . . . There are seven plane trees. I suppose they were planted one every second year, otherwise why should the seventh plane tree be the highest? Now I will go into my room and say: "Are you asleep, Mother?" What kind of a question is that! No, I'll say: "How are you, Mother?" or "Don't be hurt, ma'am . . ." No! It's impossible to say anything of the sort. This is probably the last streetcar. There it goes, and it won't be back until four o'clock in the morning. I know the conductor. He lets me get on at the front of the car. At the same time he grins as if to say: "Even though you're a great, important man, don't forget to buy a ticket."

The streetcar passed—Ding! Ding! Ding!

The clock in the university tower points to one o'clock on the side I can see. Probably day is breaking on the other side. Now I will enter the room and say something. But what? I don't know. Perhaps she will say something to me.

I opened the door carefully. My mother was lying with her hands under her head, staring at the ceiling. I went to my bed and lay down. Did I lie there for an hour, for a minute or two, or for twelve years? I remembered the past from the day she left up to today. I closed my eyes and everything appeared to me as clear as those seven plane trees, but my mother was not there. I was alone or with other people; I was everywhere and with everyone, but my mother was nowhere.

Now she and I were in one room. It was no dream. It was as real as the seven plane trees in front of the university.

Now we lay in opposite corners of the room, equally unhappy because the happy day of our re-union had come.

My God! Won't she ever speak? Probably, I shall have to say something!

"Teymuri!" I heard a low voice say. "Teymuri! Teymo!"

I could not make a sound, because my heart was in my throat.

My mother stood up. She wore a long white night-gown, and looked like a phantom as she approached my bed. She came and knelt beside me. I closed my eyes. Her trembling hand touched my temple.

"Teymuri, my little boy. Teymo, Teymiko, answer me, say something, my child!"

I wished I were dead or deaf. I wanted to scream, to call the neighbors for help.

"Teymuri, how big you are, my son. How you have grown! Who raised you, my son? Do you know you will be twenty years old tomorrow? Why aren't you still eight years old, my little one?"

She dropped her head on my breast and began to cry. I got up and lifted her to her feet. With one arm around her shoulder, I led her back to her bed.

"Why? Why?" she repeated.

"Calm yourself, if you can, I beg you."

Finally, though it was very difficult for me, I man-aged to say a few comforting words. My mother, a little more composed now, covered her face with her hands.

I returned to my bed, then looked back at her. She was sitting in the same position. I dressed and quietly left the room.

I went down through the Varasi ravine to the Vera River, and continued along a path as far as the Griffin Bridge. The street was deserted. There was one light on the top floor of a tall building, but even that light, as though bewitched, went out as soon as I looked at it. A policeman was whistling somewhere beyond the Cheluskin Bridge, officially announcing nightfall to the world. He stopped a while and started whistling again, this time, so it seemed, as though he wanted everyone to be careful and reasonable.

Silence reigned. The river made a pleasant sound, making the silence more complete.

I crossed the square and came to a grocery store. The watchman, wrapped in a sheepskin coat, was sitting on the step in front of the big door.

A single-barreled gun lay across his lap and he was warming his hands over the blazing coals of a brazier.

As I came closer he glanced at me out of one eye, without raising his head.

"Are you cold, uncle?" I said.

"I am hot!" he replied shortly, and stirred the coals with a little charcoal stick.

"May I warm myself here?"

"No, you may not!"

"Why?"

"I don't know! It isn't possible! Go away!" The old man was decidedly abrupt.

I walked back and forth in front of him. Then I stopped and said: "So you are saying it is impossible?"

"I don't say so; the law says so!" he replied, and this time he deigned to lift his head.

"I think you are exaggerating somewhat," I observed, and continued to watch him.

"What do you want, my son? Are you trying to pick a quarrel? Go away, I'm busy. You've had too much to drink. Can't you find some other place?"

"I haven't had anything to drink, old man. I simply wanted to talk to you!"

"Go away!"

Again I walked up and down, and stopped in front of him. The watchman reached under his collar and pulled out a whistle tied to his neck with a piece of rope.

"I will count up to three, and if you don't go away, I'll whistle!" he warned me.

He put the whistle in his mouth and puffed out his cheeks.

"Wait, man! What's the matter with you? Do you think I'm a thief?" I said quickly.

"One—" he began.

"Aren't you ashamed? What are you scared of?" I asked. I turned my pockets inside out. "You see, I don't have any weapons. All I want is somebody to talk to. I'll go away if you want me to." I put on a very injured expression, and prepared to leave. "Good-bye." I undid one button of my overcoat and then buttoned it up again.

"Well, go away, if you really are going! What kind of fool am I talking to?" he said.

"So you are afraid of me?" I jeered at him.

"Why should I be afraid of you? I have a gun and I have a whistle too!" the old man replied, and he seemed to be hurt.

"Some gun! It can break an iron rail with one shot, I suppose!"

"Stand forty paces back from here, and then you'll see!" the watchman taunted me.

I turned around, counted forty paces and stopped in the middle of the square. I faced the old man, bared my breast and prepared for death, like a captured partisan. I couldn't see the old man's eyes, but I knew he thought I was a madman.

"Come on, you old woman!" I shouted. It was my last insult.

The old man got up slowly, quietly, and walked to the edge of the street. He cocked the trigger, raised the gun to his shoulder, rested his cheek on the stock and aimed straight at my forehead.

"Are you crazy!" I shouted, scared to death. I ran zigzag toward the old man.

Meanwhile, the old man had put down his gun and was leaning on the barrel with both hands, shaking with laughter. I was angry.

"You are a crazy man, my friend," I said.

The old one kept on giggling. It was a hopeless task, and I sat down near the door. Finally having satisfied his heart with laughter, he came over and sat beside me.

"What are you laughing at?" I exploded.

"Were you afraid, you monkey?" he asked, and again he nearly choked with laughter.

"Do you have any tobacco?" I said, and looked away.

The old man looked at me for a long time, took a tobacco pouch from his pocket, stretched and stood up. I rolled a cigarette and gave him back the pouch. He took it and rolled a cigarette for himself, all the time looking at me. I exhaled the smoke, and he sat down.

"You could have told me from the beginning that you wanted a cigarette," he said.

I swallowed the smoke and then threw my cigarette into the brazier.

Surprised, the old man watched the cigarette burn. He shook his head and sighed.

"Something is wrong with you!"

I did not answer.

"Don't you smoke?"

"Yes," I answered.

"Why did you throw it away?"

"I don't know."

"Was it bad?"

"No, good."

The old man fell silent again.

"What day is today?" he asked suddenly.

"Monday."

"Monday is a bad day, and so is Saturday," he said.

"Why Saturday?"

"On Saturday in the district of Elia . . . Do you know Kola?"

"No, I don't."

"He is a watchman, like me."

"Oh."

"So, on Saturday in the district of Elia . . . What time is it now?"

"About four o'clock."

"At two o'clock, two young men like you came up to Kola. He is a guard, but he has only a little shop to watch, and mine is a big grocery. Well, they came up, and just like you, they asked for tobacco. Kola took out some tobacco, and just as I did with you, he gave it to them. They took it and threw the tobacco in his eyes. Before Kola could clean his eyes, they put a gag in his mouth and took away his gun, only his gun is a Geko and mine is a Central. Then they told him, 'Don't make any noise or we'll kill you!' Kola thought, 'How can anyone talk with a gag in his mouth?' But he remained silent."

"And then what?"

"Then what? They broke into the store and afterward they hit Kola a few times. 'Son of a bitch!' they said. 'The store is empty! What the devil are you doing here?' Kola thought: 'If the store were full, who would trust me to guard it?' But he remained silent."

"Did they take anything?" I asked.

"They took a scale, and ten weights, from a hundred grams to three kilograms. They also took a large mirror which was hanging in the director's room."

"What happened afterward?"

"Now, unless the thieves can be caught, Kola has to pay for whatever they stole."

"What do the police say?"

"I don't know what the police say, but Kola says that he would recognize them if they came again." The old man ended his story. As a sign of confidence he offered me the tobacco pouch again.

"Do have a smoke," he said.

I took the pouch, rolled a cigarette, and he rolled one too. We exhaled the smoke together.

"What is your first name?" he asked after a short silence.

"Teymo," I answered.

"And the last name?"

"Baramidze."

"My first name is Arthavaz. I'm an Armenian."

"Oh?"

"Yes, I'm an Armenian. What's the matter with you? Don't you have a home?" Arthavaz said. After a while he scratched his neck and looked at me out of the corner of his eye.

"Yes, I have a home."

"When a man has a home but dares not go there, that means he does not have a home!" Arthavaz said, as though speaking to himself.

"Do you have a mother?" I asked him.

"That's all I need!" he smiled.

"Have you been without her for a long time?"

"A long time."

"How old was she?"

"When she died I was sixty-one, but I don't know how old she was."

"Do you have a wife?"

"No."

"Or a son?"

"If I had a son, would I be working here?" Arthavaz said with a pained expression. I stopped talking. "What about you?" he went on after a short silence.

"About me?"

"Do you have a mother?"

"My mother came back yesterday."

"And you are walking the streets?"

"My mother came from exile."

"From where?"

"She came from prison."

"How did she get out of prison?"

"Very simple. They opened the door and she walked out."

"Blockhead! Your mother comes out of prison and you sit here with me!?"

Arthavaz stood up, and after a while sat down again.

The first streetcar of the day, squeaking and rumbling, crossed the square.

I looked up at the sky. The night was growing pale. Somewhere near the Svanethi district, a locomotive going to or from Kakhethi was whistling incessantly.

Morning was coming to Tiflis from the direction of Narikala.

"Get up!" he said. I did not move. "Get up! My work is finished. It is daybreak."

I stood up and walked toward the square.

"Where are you going, boy?"

"I don't know," I said, shrugging my shoulders.

"Wait, I'm going in that direction, too," he said. He slung his gun over his shoulder and came with me. We crossed the square and continued along Lenin Street. Arthavaz walked beside me. I slowed down when I saw that it was difficult for him to walk so fast. The chill of morning made me shiver. I turned up the collar of my raincoat and plunged my hands deep in my pockets. When we reached the police station, Arthavaz stopped. In front of the station a young policeman was trying to start a motorcycle. He kicked the starter over and over, but nothing happened. The motor would roar once, and then die again. When he saw us, he stopped balancing on one leg.

"Hey, Arthavaz! You left your post early today!" the policeman shouted from under his arm.

"Isn't it enough that I stayed this long with nothing to look at but two rats, both of which fainted from starvation?!"

"Wait here for me, I'll be right back," Arthavaz continued, and then he went into the police station.

"This son of a bitch won't start!" the policeman said, and spat at the motor.

"You can start it by rolling it down the hill," I suggested.

"But I have to go up the hill," the policeman protested.

"My dear fellow, go down first and then go up," I said.

The policeman gave me a grateful smile and rolled the motorcycle down the hill. Arthavaz came out of the police station. He had no gun. He had left it at the station.

"Who is he?" I asked, pointing at the policeman.

"A stupid fellow! Every morning it's the same thing! We'd better go!" Arthavaz said, and slapped me on the shoulder. We went.

For the whole way he did not say a word. He stopped in front of a restaurant and I stopped too.

"We go in?" Arthavaz said.

I shrugged my shoulders and closed my eyes.

"Let's go in," he repeated, and went in.

I followed. He went to the farthest table, took off his sheepskin, hung it over the back of a chair, and sat down. I sat down without taking off my coat. There was a pleasant smell of garlic, boiled meat and tobacco smoke in the cellar. Only a few tables were occupied, but more people kept coming in. A waiter came and stood before us with an air of indifference.

"Two boiled tripe, two vodkas, one lemonade!" Arthavaz ordered. The waiter wrote it down.

"The tripe must come with a hoof," Arthavaz warned him.

"A cow has only four hooves," the waiter said.

"Eight!" Arthavaz corrected him. "Now go and fetch it!"

Two minutes later Arthavaz and I were mixing garlic with the tripe.

Little by little the cellar was filling up with people with swollen faces, bloodshot eyes and red noses— they were people who came here after sleepless nights spent in carousing.

"One boiled tripe, two vodkas!"

"Another round—two glasses of high-grade spirits!"

"Waiter, is this tripe or sole?"

"Waiter! I want to make a complaint!"

"Waiter, do you have any spot-remover?"

"Son of a bitch! Am I supposed to roll dice with these bones? Bring me some meat!"

Noise surrounded us. With bored smiles the waiters carried bowls of tripe, they noisily clicked the abacus as they added up the bills, they downed a glass of vodka whenever they found a chance, they wiped their faces on their dirty sleeves and looked around with half-closed eyes. Bathed in its own sweat, the cellar groaned, sighed, laughed, bawled, staggered and breathed heavily, like a man wrapped in smoke.

"Your good health!" said old Arthavaz, and touched his glass to mine.

"Your health!" I said, and gulped down the vodka.

"Is it possible for me to sit down here?" a tall, pale, intellectual type asked us. He stood at our table, leaning with both hands on the back of the third chair.

"No, it isn't possible!" said Arthavaz.

"What?" The thin man was astonished. "Why isn't it possible?"

"Because I have typhus and he has tuberculosis!" Arthavaz pointed at me. The thin man looked at us suspiciously, and left.

"Waiter!" Arthavaz shouted. The waiter came.

"Take that chair away and come back with another two glasses of a hundred grams."

The waiter removed the chair, and returned with a whole bottle of vodka.

"I'll take back what's left over," he said, and stood at the side of the table.

Arthavaz poured, saying, "Well, my dear—"

"Teymo," I reminded him.

"Dear Teymo! To the good luck of our meeting!" he said, and he touched his glass to mine.

"Your good health!" I said, and gulped it down.

I felt the vodka run down my throat and spread through my body. It mixed with my blood, it hit all the hollows, all the cells, all the veins, then it came back, made my face warm, swelled my temples. My tired eyelids closed. The hall plunged into darkness, then the darkness thinned out and emerged from a rosy mist with a thousand white and sparkling stars. I opened my eyes. The mist dissolved. From the mist a formless face rose to the surface, and little by little I began to see a straight, slightly pockmarked nose, black eyebrows, an unshaven beard and quiet, watery, tired eyes which were large, honey-colored and peaceful below lids wrinkled with age. These quizzical eyes looked at me for a long time without blinking. They waited for me to say something. I knew that he would not speak until I did, but in spite of that I did not utter a sound. Then uncle Arthavaz poured another glass.

"With this, my Teymo, let us drink to the man who walks in the night and seeks another man. Let us drink to the man who sits in the night and waits for another man. Let us drink to all men who find no sleep at night, some because they don't want to sleep and some because they cannot, though they want to very much. In any case they both wait for the coming day. Well, blessed be the night which ends in daybreak."

Old Arthavaz drank this toast without touching his glass to my glass. He accompanied it with a spoonful of tripe, and stared at me again. I said nothing, but I drank the vodka. Old Arthavaz poured again. I realized that he would not drink unless I said something, so I raised my glass.

"You, Arthavaz, are waiting for the dawn. I am drunk now. How old are you, Arthavaz?" He was silent.

"How old are you?" I insisted.

"Two hundred."

"So you are two hundred years old, and I am twenty years old, and today is my birthday. You are two hundred years old, and you wait for daybreak, and I—Why do you look at me in that way? I'm afraid of daybreak, did you know that?! No, you don't know. I'm afraid of the dawn, I'm afraid to go home. Do you know why?"

"Well, why?" Arthavaz said. His watery eyes were brimming with tears.

"Why? Because a woman is waiting for me at home. She is sitting on the bed. She wears a white gown, a white nightgown that reaches to her ankles. She is sitting and waiting for me. Strange, strange woman! Do you know how strange she is? This woman is my mother. I haven't seen her in twelve whole years. Now she expects me to call her Mother, and I can't do that, do you understand? Because I'm ashamed! No, I'm not ashamed, I'm afraid! Or rather . . . no, I am not afraid. I've grown out of the habit. Do you understand?"

Old Arthavaz nodded his head.

"Well, that's that!" I said, coming to the end of my oration, and I took a drink.

Arthavaz looked at me for a long time, then raised his glass.

"I drink to the health and victory of the mother who did not see her son for twelve whole years, but sat in prison all that time and waited and did not lose heart. In spite of everything she found her cub and found her son. Victory to that mother who doesn't sleep at night, not because she doesn't want to sleep, but because she cannot. She waits for daybreak. Blessed be the night which brings the dawn!"

Arthavaz gulped down his vodka. I took the bottle. Arthavaz covered my glass with his palm.

"You don't need any more," he said.

I put down the bottle.

"Waiter!" he shouted.

The waiter came.

"The check!"

"Ninety rubles," the waiter said, without blushing. Arthavaz gave him a hundred rubles, and stood up.

"Thank you," the waiter smiled at him.

"Enjoy it!" Arthavaz inclined his head, and began putting on his sheepskin.

The restaurant was empty. Cleaning women were clearing the tables. I stood up, too. I was completely drunk. In order not to fall, I held Arthavaz's arm. He carefully led me up to the stairs and propped me against a plane tree.

"Can you walk?" he said.

"Yes."

"Then go on your way, but walk slowly."

"Arthavaz, won't you come with me?"

"Where, my boy?"

"With me!"

"With you? Yes, but not today. Some other day."

"Now!"

"No, now I must go to Kukia."

"What do you have to do in Kukia?"

"I'm going to visit my mother's grave," he said.

"I will go with you."

"You go home, and I will go to Kukia."

"Arthavaz!"

"What now?"

"I want to kiss you good-bye."

Arthavaz came up to me, wiped his lips on his

hand, and kissed me on the forehead. Before I could kiss him, he turned and went away. He was bending as he walked, swaying, dragging his feet heavily. He was probably drunk. He crossed the street. When he reached the pharmacy, he looked back. I stood where he had left me, and looked at him. Arthavaz waved his hand, then turned and walked toward the Vera.

I moved away from the plane tree and walked along the sidewalk. The alcohol hurled me from side to side: first I banged against a wall and then into a tree. I stopped. This is shameful. I must try to walk straight, straight, quite evenly to that tree. It's better to take fast steps. I started walking. I reached the tree. Now to the next tree. There were very few people on the street. It was still quite early.

"Excuse me! What time is it?" I stopped someone.

"Seven!" he answered without even glancing at his watch.

I was not hurt at all. Either he knew the time by heart, or else he was cheating me to get rid of me. Possibly he had no watch, and so what? I do the same thing when some drunk stops me.

"Excuse me. Do you have any cigarettes?" I stopped a second person.

He sighed, and quickly offered me a pack of cigarettes. He must have matches too, but he is in a hurry. Even if I ask him, he probably won't light one for me. Never mind, I will stop someone else.

"Thank you, sir!" I bowed my head.

"Not at all, not at all!" he shouted as he ran off.

I reached Melikishvili Street. The merchants had already begun to open the shops.

"Excuse me, do you have a match?" I asked someone who was unlocking his doors and removing sealing wax. Without a word he took a flat box of matches from his pocket and offered it to me. I lit the cigarette and returned the matches.

"Keep it. I have more," he said, and opened the door of his shop.

"Thank you," I said and went on.

This is the front door of my house. One step, two, three, four, five, six . . . I wish I knew how many steps there are. I have never counted them in my life. But how can I say that! Did I do anything else when I was a child? But I don't remember. I must go back and count again. One, two, three, four, five, six, seven, eight, nine, ten, eleven . . . Eleven steps. I live on the fourth floor, so this means eight times eleven. How much is eight times eleven? Eight times eleven is a lot. You must walk a lifetime, all of your life, to reach the end. Eight times eleven. I pressed my finger to the doorbell, but even before it rang, the door opened. There stood my mother, gray and pretty, as pretty as she was twelve years ago when she was the most beautiful mother in the world.

"How do you do, my mother?" I said.

My mother stood at the door. She did not cry, she smiled, and hot tears streamed down her cheeks and clung to her trembling chin.

"How do you do, my mother?" I said again.

Gulika

On Lotkin Hill it is still spring, but in Tiflis the hot scorching summer reigns. Tiflis burns, melts, the asphalt evaporates. The blazing sun walks on the tin roofs, looks in the windows, and then hangs over the city for such a long time that you think it will never leave. The Mtkvari River dries up and finally becomes so shallow that you can cross the riverbed on foot. It is summer now in Tiflis, and it is impossible to stay in the house.

I got up before the sun was too high. My mother was already in the kitchen, boiling water for tea. When she saw me she poured the colored liquid into a glass.

"Go, open the door, my son," she said.

I opened the door. Guram came straight into the kitchen without bothering to look around.

"How are you, Aunt Anika?" he said, and sat down before the glass of tea.

"How are you, my boy?"

"Do you know, Teymo, that Churchill is rattling a lot of weapons!" he said, frowning.

"You can't be serious!"

"If you don't believe me, just listen to the radio," he smiled ironically.

"What did the radio say?"

"The radio said Churchill was rattling his saber."

"And then what?"

"Then nothing! A man who takes up a weapon and doesn't use it is a disgrace forever!"

He made that statement as if he were a professional rifleman.

"Against whom is he rattling his saber, my boy?" Mother asked.

"He is rattling it against us, Aunt Anika, against us!" Guram stressed the final word.

"So you want a war? Isn't it enough that we have to stand in line for oil and bread?" I said, and swallowed a mouthful of tea.

"I don't want a war. What I want is the ruin of the whole world!" he said angrily.

"Why?"

"Because, Comrade Baramidze, I can't take any more of this tension—sitting like an utter fool during examinations, worrying about my lost scholarship, having trembling knees and a choked-up throat, breathing my last while dreaming of a 'C.' In any case I can't possibly take the examinations in statistics, and if a war must begin, let it begin now! I accuse Churchill of standing in the way of my taking the exams. Also, my father's sneering will kill me."

"What is he saying now?"

"He says 'My son, I have no right to blame you

for anything. I have ruined you. If I had sent you to the school for the retarded, you would have won a gold medal by now.' "

"Would you? I'm not so sure."

"You are joking. Do you know how easy it is to study there? For example: You arrive at the exams; the wall is covered with pictures—an apple, a pear, a peach. You come to the exams and the examiner says, 'Now, Baramidze, pay close attention, don't hurry, think carefully and answer me. What is this?' and he puts his hand on the apple. You look closely at the apple, and answer: 'It is an apple, sir.' 'Bravo, bravo, Baramidze!' the happy professor says, and gives you an 'A.' If you mistake the apple for a pear, you get a 'B,' and if you mistake it for a peach, then a 'C.' "

"And if you say it's a compote?"

"For a brilliant answer like that you will be made a research student!"

"And when do they ever give an 'F'?" I asked, laughing.

"They give an 'F' if you say the apple is a streetcar."

"If that's so, of course you would be the winner of the gold medal, my son," my mother assured him.

All three of us exploded with laughter. We finished our tea. I took out the course synopses.

"Will you be back soon?" my mother asked us.

"We have to work all day," Guram replied.

Quickly we ran downstairs. We took the number 5 streetcar as far as the covered market without having paid for a ticket; we continued on the number 10, again without a ticket. We got off near Nadsaladevi and then we climbed up Lotkin Hill where it was still spring, where there was a little house with a little courtyard, a spurred rooster, a vicious dog and some shade, where dear, good Gulika lived.

Gulika is my classmate. When Tiflis is boiling, Guram and I study with her. Aside from the fact that

Gulika's courtyard is cool, and Guram and I like to study with her, she is assigned by the Communist Youth Committee to see that the students' "C's" outweigh their "D's." Guram and I have known from the first year that there is no highway to the summits of knowledge, but only a narrow path. Because of that we were now listening to Gulika, who described so artistically how a worm, discovered in the borsch, led to the rebellion on the battle cruiser *Potemkin* that my mouth watered from pleasure.

Gulika reads the synopsis. From time to time she looks up to see if we are listening. Guram sits with his head resting on the round table, his chin on one fist and his eyes half-closed. It is difficult to know whether he is dozing or listening to her. I lean my back against the plum tree and cannot take my eyes off Gulika's pretty little head around which the rising sun creates a halo, lighting up the golden hair falling over her shoulders.

"Gulika!" I say, and I myself do not know why.

"What?" she replies, without raising her head.

"Nothing."

"Well, what?"

"Move, otherwise the sun will set your hair on fire!" I smile at her.

"That's not very funny!" says Gulika, and she continues to read.

Guram opened one eye like a lazy cat, took a cigarette out of his pocket, and signaled to me for a match. I pointed at Gulika's head. Guram stood up lazily, planted the cigarette in Gulika's fiery hair, and inhaled deeply.

"It doesn't catch fire," he said and shrugged his shoulders.

"Stop clowning!" Gulika said angrily. She passed her hand over her hair.

"If you don't want to listen to this, don't! I myself have read this outline three times!"

"My life for Gulika! For darling, good, kind, pretty,

talented Gulika! We have had enough study and education. Let's take a walk somewhere!" Guram said, his
voice full of emotion.

"Do you agree?" Gulika asked me.

"I have had the same idea for a long time, but I
couldn't say it, any more than I can confess my love
for you."

Gulika smiled and closed the book.

"Mother!" she called to Aunt Thamar, who was
busy indoors.

"What do you want, my child?" her mother said,
coming out.

"Mother, the boys are leaving and I am going with
them. Don't worry if I'm late."

"Well, then go, my dear," her mother said. "Have you
studied the long outline so quickly?" Aunt Thamar
asked, somewhat surprised.

"You can ask me anything you want!" a slightly
hurt Guram replied, and he prepared to answer any
questions she asked him.

"What can I ask you? I've never even looked at it!"
said Aunt Thamar.

"That is not very good, not good at all, my dear.
I'm afraid you will not go very far. Look into it,
read it, and come back in the fall!" advised Guram,
and went to the gate.

"We're going, Mother," said Gulika, and took my
arm.

"Go, my child, don't be too late!"

If you look down from the funicular at night, Tiflis resembles a starry sky. It is as if the sky had descended,
turned itself face upward, and you were looking down
at it from above. All the known stars and satellites
lie beneath you: the Big and Little Bears, the Scale,
Mars and the Milky Way spread a mist of light. Far
away, like falling stars, automobile lights blaze and dis-
appear. The funicular is like the earth, swimming in the
cosmos, with the sky below, sky above, sky every-

where, on every side. Sky infinite, limitless, studded with
endless stars, on and on. You yourself are the earth, the
little earth, breathing, thinking, dreaming, lost and
wandering. This earth is your twin, partaking of your
pains and joys, seeking the living earth in this awesome
commotion of stars.

I don't know what Gulika is thinking about now.
She leans on the balustrade and looks at Tiflis. I don't
care what Guram thinks about, but I do care about
Gulika's thoughts. I wish Gulika would think the
same things that I do, or if not exactly the same, at
least similar. How many times have I dreamed, oh
God, of asking her if she thinks about the same
thing as I, but I have never dared, up to today. Now
I think: if Guram will invent some excuse and will
start to leave, Gulika will ask him to remain. Nevertheless, Guram will go. Then Gulika will say she
has to go, and I'll ask her to stay and she will stay.
Then I will tell Gulika everything. I will tell her
that I have loved her for two years, that I think about
her all the time, that perhaps she does not love me,
but that is not important. But it is impossible that Gulika should not love me. I have noticed that she loves
me very much. At least I think she does.

"I'm going now!" Guram said suddenly. "I have to
get up early tomorrow morning. I have to go and buy
some oil."

"Wait a while and we'll go back together," I said.

"I can't," Guram said.

"If you can't, then go on. Teymuri and I will
stay here, won't we?" Gulika said.

"Of course. How can we possibly go back to Tiflis?"

"Well, I'm going. Good-bye!"

"Good-bye."

"Come by in the morning!"

"All right."

Guram left.

Now I look at Gulika and Gulika looks at Tiflis.

Now I think only of Gulika and I wish I knew what she was thinking. Oh God, I will ask her now, and if she is thinking about something else, never in my life will I ask her again.

"Teymo!"

"What is it, Gulika?"

"Teymo, what are you thinking about?" Gulika said, and looked into my eyes.

I opened my mouth in surprise. Gulika did not take her eyes off me.

"Nothing, Gulika! What should I be thinking about?" I squeezed out the words with difficulty.

Gulika smiled slightly and looked away.

"What are you thinking?"

"What am I thinking? I'm thinking about you," Gulika said and smiled again.

"Now? At this very minute?"

"Now, at this very minute!"

"What else do you think about, Gulika?" I asked, with a catch in my voice.

"I think about myself, too, Teymo."

"What else?"

"Nothing else. When I think about you, I think of myself too, and nothing else. Probably I'm not intelligent enough to think of anything else."

"Do you think of me at other times, too?"

"Yes."

"Often?"

"Often."

"Very much?"

"No!" Gulika was now standing near the parapet, her head bent, looking at her thin and transparent fingers.

I was afraid, and didn't ask her anything, but Gulika herself said, "Sometimes I think, Teymo, for a very long time."

I moved nearer to Gulika. My arm touched her arm. I felt it tremble, but she did not move away.

"Gulika!"

Gulika looked directly into my eyes. I could not bear it, so I looked aside.

"Gulika, what do you think about me?" I asked in a trembling voice, and I closed my eyes, waiting for her answer.

"The same as you think about me," Gulika said in a low voice.

My heart came up to my throat and I could not breathe. I put my arm around her. She took my hand between her shoulder and her cheek, rested her head on it and closed her eyes.

"Gulika, do you know what I think of you? Now I'll tell you everything . . ."

Gulika did not open her eyes, but waved her hand to show that I should be silent. But I could not stop. It was as though I were a stone rolling down a mountain—a boulder which had hung for years by a thread and then, once loosened, brings everything down with it, everything in its path, a landslide, a snowslide, an avalanche.

"I'll go to the sea this summer. No, first I'll go to the Lebai Mountains, to herd sheep. Then to the sea. Maybe I'll go to camp, too. I like the sea more than anything—sea and sun, sun and sea. They are two miracles. Aren't they miracles? Of course they are! I can sit on the shore, my back to the sea, and look at the sunrise, then turn around and watch the sun set directly into the sea, then wait for the sun to rise and set, and so on for the rest of my life.

"This year you and I will go together to the sea. I will put my head in your lap and look at you for the whole day. You may look at whatever you wish—the sea, the sun—only don't look at me! When you look at me I am afraid. At the same time I am glad. That is why I prefer to look at you. But occasionally you may gaze at me. Well, Gulika? We will go to the sea together, won't we?"

"Yes, Teymuri. Yes," Gulika whispered, and opened her eyes a little. I turned her toward me, ran both hands through her fiery hair and drew her to me. In her wide-open eyes I saw tears and, mixed with the tears, limitless happiness, love and something unknown to me. I was afraid of the unknown thing. To extinguish this fear, I kissed her eyes—carefully, again and again.

Afterward everything fell back into its usual place. Tiflis still sparkled below, strangely similar to the sky turned face upward. Above there was the same limitless sky, studded with large and small stars. Everywhere there was sky, sky without beginning, without end. And I was the earth, the little earth, breathing, thinking, living, dreaming, tormented, saved, infinitely happy. And by my side there stood, equal in all my pains and loves, the bearer of the love and pain, the living earth, and I was not alone in this awesome commotion of stars.

The Mother

I opened the door. My mother was sitting near the window and looking out at the Varasi ravine. She always waited for me, no matter what time I came in. She waited with silent, sad, reproachful eyes. I felt as though I committed some crime when I went out without telling her, but I could not behave otherwise. During twelve whole years no one had asked me when I would return, and now when I was asked I became terribly angry. Sometimes I purposely came home late, and sometimes not at all. My mother felt this, and, with the passing of time, she became sadder and more silent. Often I spent sleepless nights, and so did she. Finally I would fall asleep, and when at last I awoke, I would see her staring at me sadly. She never

45

asked me about anything, nor told me about anything. And I neither asked nor told her anything. But today was different. If I had had no one to talk to, I would have spoken to the wall, to a stone, a tree, to anyone and anything.

I went up to my mother, sat beside her, put my hands on her lap and looked into her wise, honey-colored eyes.

"What is it, son?" she asked me, and stroked my head with her hand.

"Mother, do you remember the sea? I remember you once took me to Kobuleti when I was a child."

"I remember, son," she said.

My mother looked at me with surprise.

"Aren't the sea and the sun two miracles? The sun is such a miracle that you could not possibly grow tired of staring at it. Don't you think so, Mother?"

"No, son," my mother said, closing her eyes and shaking her head. She was silent for a long time. Probably she was remembering something.

"Mother!" I said.

"Yes, the sun is a miracle," she began after a silence, "But you have never seen the real sun. The endless plains burned by the sun. Stone, earth, trees, sand, scorched by the sun, parched mouth, bruised brain. There are moments in life when you hate the sun, and you look at the sunset only because you are glad the sun is going down. And you wish that the cruel sun would never rise again. Do you understand, my son?"

I said nothing. My mother smiled sadly.

"The sun you love is really a miracle, and you will never tire of looking at it until the day you die." Having said this, she stroked my wet forehead with her hot hand. I put my head on her lap.

"Mother, can't you see that I'm no longer a little boy? You think I'm still eight years old, but I'm more than twenty. You are troubled by everything I do . . . You don't like the things I like; and you are afraid of the things I enjoy. You are always suspicious. Either you must forget everything about my past, or else you must tell me what to do," I said, and kissed the hem of her dress.

"It is impossible to forget such things," my mother said.

"You mean, you still think I am eight years old?" I raised my head and looked into her eyes.

"Yes," she said, and her chin began to tremble.

"Why, Mother? Why?"

"Because in my mind and memory my child has never grown up."

"And yet you know very well I am not eight years old—I am twenty."

"That doesn't mean anything to me," my mother said, and smiled bitterly.

"What? I, today . . . today . . ." I stammered.

"What about today?" she said, quietly.

"Today, I told Gulika that I loved her more than the whole world, and we are going to stay by the sea, and I will put my head in her lap and from morning to evening we will watch the sun rise and set—that sun which you don't like—and we shall be together all our lives. Does this mean anything to you?"

My mother stood up, pressed my head to her breast with one hand and with the other she began to stroke my hair, all the while whispering, "It means, my son, it means, my Teymuri, it means everything, only you must stay with me, be my son, don't be a stranger to me. Do you hear? A stranger! And then I will forget all that happened. Only say to me, too, what you said to Gulika. Tell me, son, that you love me, that we will be together for a lifetime. Otherwise you will break my poor heart!"

My mother sank into a chair and covered her face with her hands. There was a lump in my throat, but I controlled myself and sat down before her again, putting my hands on the hem of her skirt. My mother did not cry, but her hands trembled. After a while, she was quiet and took her hands away from her face.

"Mother," I began, "I have been in love with Gulika now for two years. Can you imagine! Two years . . ."

"That is not too much, my child," my mother said, and she smiled at me. I could not say anything for a while.

"I love you very much, too," I said timidly.

"I know," my mother said, and smiled again.

"Only . . ."

"You love Gulika more than you love me, and you want to be with her always?" she interrupted.

"No!"

"Yes!"

"I love Gulika in another way. I fell in love with Gulika only recently, and you . . . I have loved you for such a long time . . ."

"A very very long time—so long that even you have forgotten!"

"Mother, did you love my father?" I asked suddenly.

My mother closed her eyes and did not answer. I realized I had said something stupid.

"Do you remember your father?" my mother asked me after a while.

I began to think. Oh God! Is it possible that I don't remember? I remember he had two gold teeth on one side of his mouth, he was of medium height, handsome, black-haired—so black that it seemed almost blue. He wore a leather overcoat, sometimes he wore boots, sometimes narrow shoes and narrow trousers. He was a stern man, and when people wanted something from him, they always asked me first. He loved me very much. What else? Nothing else. My eyes are closed and I try to picture this man—my father. I see nothing, only emptiness, absolute emptiness. Everything I know has been told to me by others. I don't remember anything, and the more I try to remember, the more impossible it becomes.

"No, Mother, I don't remember. Absolutely nothing. I thought I remembered . . ."

"Haven't you seen his picture?"

"No."

My mother went to the cupboard, took out a photograph and set it before me. I stared at it, then I looked up at my mother. She was pale and silent. I took the picture in my hand. There was a happy, smiling, one-year-old baby rolling on a bear rug.

"Who is it?" I asked, a little frightened.

"It is your father. They thought it was your picture, and so they let me take it with me," my mother said.

"And then?" I said. The photograph gave me the shivers.

"Then nothing. That is your father, and I am your mother."

I threw the photograph on the table. Then I went to my mother, leaned my head on her shoulder and began to cry. My mother was silent. She didn't try to comfort me. She said nothing.

"Mother, forgive me, my poor mother!" I began, and I clenched my teeth to prevent myself from sobbing. "Forgive me for the suffering I have caused you. Forgive me—me and Father too. Mother, I will do anything for you. If you wish, I will even kill someone! If you want me to leave Gulika or kill myself, I will do it! I will do anything you say—tell me, only forgive me, forgive me!" I was crying and kissing her.

My mother stroked my head without speaking. Then, as if she remembered something, she said slowly, "I don't ask you for anything. I don't want you to kill yourself for my sake, nor to kill anyone else. Don't say such things. Why should you leave

Gulika? Love her, if you love her and she loves you too. At your age you don't know what love is, and you probably won't know for a long time to come. My life is not yet ended, but it seems that my road is ended. I will accompany you on your road as long as I live, to see that you remain true and honest. Perhaps you will need a helping hand and I will give it to you. You have your fate, and you must go your own way, my son."

"How, Mother, how?"

"I don't know, son. If I knew that, we should not have any worries."

"But what are we supposed to do?"

"Everything that is good and honest."

"What else?"

"I don't know, son. Sometimes one commits evil, thinking to do good."

My mother fell silent; I too became quiet. She went to the window and gazed down at the Varasi ravine. I came and stood beside her. She understood that I was waiting for her to say something more. She turned and smiled at me.

"The first thing you must learn is to make the distinction between good and evil."

"How, Mother?"

"I don't know," she shrugged. "Life itself will teach you."

"And what should I do now?"

"Now?" my mother grew pensive. "Now go and lie down," she said, and kissed me on the forehead.

Wordlessly, I turned around and went to bed. In the morning when I woke up, my mother was still sitting at the window, her head resting on her arm, smiling and sleeping sweetly. Silently I put on my clothes, took my books and opened the door.

"Are you up, my child?" I heard her voice.

I turned to her and smiled.

"Where are you going?" she asked me.

To my great surprise, for the first time in my life I felt glad that someone asked me where I was going, and was interested in my coming and going. And for fear of losing the warmth and intimacy of her words, I remained at home.

Parnassus

———

There were about three thousand students in the university. Of that number one half studied, one fourth waited for their diplomas, while the rest chose various professions, changed faculties, wrote manifestos, went on academic leaves, brought certificates of illness to their examinations, came and went like the wind, wrestled, played, sang and so on. We, the literati, belonged to an official literary club whose leader was a certain Shalva. The membership included about five critics, twenty poets, six prose writers, two essayists and nine translators.

I was a poet, but sometimes in secret I wrote short stories. We met every Friday in lecture hall number

52

94, and there shared the results of the week's crea-
tive work which had been squeezed out by the sweat
of our brows. First we discussed it with the members
and then read it in the presence of the leader. The
best work was read later at a literary party which
was held once a month. And there, in the vaulted
clubhouse completely filled with students who were
devotees of poetry, we showered the audience with
the pearls of our imagination and skill.

Guram never missed a meeting. It is true that he
was neither poet, nor novelist, nor essayist, nor critic,
nor translator, but he called himself, fondly, a "dilet-
tante," and he helped me to find rhymes for my
verses.

Today is Friday. Guram and I sit in the last row
and wait for the lecture hall to fill with the forty
geniuses, who, with half-closed eyes, enter as though
they were in deep thought, forget to greet us, and
then apologize. "Uh, so you are here? I didn't notice
you. I was somewhere else . . ." and so on.

"Hey, Erecle!" Guram called to a red-haired poet
who carried a whole library of books under his arm.
He sat down just in front of us and stared at the
ceiling as if it were about to fall down.

Erecle did not move.

"Hey, Erecle!" Guram shook him. "I know you're
far away, but please come back for a moment if you
possibly can."

Erecle quivered, called his scattered thoughts to
order, and annihilated us with a glance of his myopic
eyes.

"Oh, are you here? How could I not have noticed
you?" he wondered.

"Where were you?" Guram asked.

"I came from home," Erecle answered in a tired
voice.

"No, where were you just now?" Guram insisted.

"At this moment?" Erecle replied to Guram's question with another question.

Once more an expression of inspiration started to come over his face, but Guram stopped him.

"Yes, at this very moment, when you were looking at the ceiling. Where were you?"

"I was thinking about something."

"About what?"

"Why did you bother me when I was thinking about other things?" Erecle became angry.

"Were you thinking about a poem?"

"No."

"Were you trying to find a rhyme?"

"How did you know?" Erecle said, surprised.

"Tell me about it. I am here to help!" Guram joyfully slapped him on the shoulder.

"I am composing a poem cycle about the electric plant at Samgori."

"Did you get stuck?"

"No, I didn't get stuck, but I can't find a rhyme."

"What kind of a rhyme do you want?" Guram swallowed in anticipation of a fat morsel.

"Mephistopheles!" Erecle said.

Guram was taken aback.

"Did it just hit you?" Guram asked Erecle and smiled at him gently, like a nurse smiling at a patient.

"Every poet is hit in his own way," Erecle said significantly, and opened his eyes wide.

Guram now smiled at me as before he had smiled at Erecle.

"Stop grinning and find a rhyme for him, if you can!" I objected angrily.

"What has Mephistopheles to do with Samgori?" Guram said.

"Yes, what does Mephistopheles have to do with Samgori?" I repeated.

Erecle was not in this world. Again he had gone somewhere, was fixedly staring at the ceiling and murmuring to himself: "Mephistopheles, Mephistopheles, Mephistopheles . . ."

"Look here!" Guram tugged at Erecle's sleeve. "Read the verse aloud!"

Erecle began to recite:

> "And there was a severe drought in Samgori
> As in hell, Mephistopheles . . ."

"*Mephis tuphli (the king's slippers)*," Guram suggested.

"It doesn't fit," Erecle shook his head.

"*Chveni sopheli (our village)*," Guram tried again.

"I can't use that!" Erecle had no pity for him.

"*Bevr kitrs movelith (we expect many cucumbers)*," Guram refused to give up.

"I have cucumber in the previous verse!" Erecle waved a hand.

"*Mephis staphilo (the king's carrot)*."

"The carrot is good, but the king doesn't convey anything!"

"*Marto staphilo (the only carrot)*."

"The only carrot doesn't convey anything."

"*Meti staphilo (more carrots)*."

"No!"

"*Mash, idioti (well, idiot)*."

"It doesn't rhyme!"

"But it rhymes with you, you imbecile! Couldn't you compare a drought to something besides Mephistopheles?" Guram got mad, and jumped to his feet.

Erecle looked at Guram in such a way that I felt sorry for him. "That's enough now!" I said, and made Guram sit down.

The lecture hall was full.

Suddenly the door opened and Zurab Chkheidze entered the room. He was a doctoral candidate in the department of language and literature, who hoped someday to be a professor of philology.

When illness or lack of time kept Shalva from a meeting, Zurab replaced our chief. Like Guram,

Zurab never missed a meeting. Usually he sat in the last row and listened attentively to the rest of us. He never expressed an opinion, and for that reason we did not think much of him.

"How are you?" he said in a weak voice. He removed his glasses, breathed on them, polished them with his handkerchief, put them on again and sat down.

"How are you?"

"Greetings."

"Victory to you!" we greeted him, without enthusiasm.

"Shall we begin?" he said.

"Shouldn't we wait for Comrade Shalva?" Guram demanded.

Guram knew Zurab better than the rest of us. He even drank beer with him occasionally.

"Shalva is ill, my dear Guram. But he telephoned me and asked me to conduct the meeting today in his place."

"In that case we can begin," Guram said. Zurab smiled. "By the way, how are you, Mr. Zurab?" Guram went on, growing bolder.

"So so, thank you. And how are you?"

"I have no reason to be sorrowful!" Guram said, in the best literary Georgian.

"Is anything wrong with you?" Zurab asked.

"Absolutely not!

"What happened? Is your hair falling out?" Zurab anxiously passed his hand over Guram's head.

"What is the matter with you? My hair is all right!" Guram was surprised.

"Nothing wrong with it?"

"No."

"That's perfect! What are you doing? Are you writing poems?"

"No."

"Prose?"

"Not prose, either."

"Are you translating anything?"

"No!"

"No critical articles?"

"No."

"What is the matter? Everyone else writes! Why don't you? Write something!"

"Yes, sir."

"Very well! Now we can begin. Whose poems shall we hear today?"

"Mine!" exclaimed Erecle, returning from his distant thoughts. He stood up.

"Come forward," Zurab said.

Erecle mounted the rostrum. He laid his hand on a notebook, just as witnesses in court used to lay their hands on the Gospel, saying: "God punish me if I tell a lie!" Then he stared up at the ceiling. A tomblike silence fell in the hall. Erecle said nothing; the audience too was silent. I counted up to sixty and still that stupid man did not begin.

"Sixty-one, sixty-two, sixty-three . . ." I continued counting.

"Will you begin?" Zurab said, interrupting my count.

Erecle was silent.

"He is waiting for his muse!" Guram explained.

"If he would only begin, the muse would come of herself. How could she possibly leave him in the lurch?" Zurab said.

A burst of laughter from the audience seemed to awaken Erecle, who again returned from far away.

He began: "A week ago, having left my house, I hurried to the newsstand and asked for a newspaper . . ."

"Is this going to be a novel?" Zurab said, alarmed.

"An introduction," Erecle said heavily.

"Why does a poem need an introduction? Barathashvili's 'Pegasus' has no preface! It begins directly: 'My horse flies, and carries me aimlessly on its wings. . . .' Isn't that right, Guram?"

"Yes," Guram confirmed his opinion.

"Barathashvili and I are not the same person!" Erecle explained.

"Indeed, there is a difference," Zurab commented.

The audience exploded with so much laughter that the windowpanes trembled.

"Are you laughing at me? Do you know what was written in the newspaper?" Erecle glowered.

"Well, what was written in it?"

"That Samgori is a part of the great constructive cycle of Communism!"

"Erecle, you bought a year-old newspaper! Why are you shouting at us about an article that was published last year?" Zurab asked.

Erecle was stupefied. He looked again at the newspaper, which he had brought with him. He seemed stunned.

Zurab noticed that Erecle was unhappy, so he encouraged him.

"Never mind!" he said. "Tell us what happened after you read the article."

"I wrote a cycle of poems about Samgori," Erecle said.

"Well, read it to us!"

Silence fell again. I began to count again: One, two, three . . . and then a miracle happened. Erecle began:

THE MORNING OF SAMGORI

Here a drought had laid its hands,
The wind stretched, trembling,
The hills of Samgori were silent.
It is a miracle! Is it not?

Soon, soon on the scorched plain
We shall have great heaps
Of red tomatoes.
You are lucky, O Samgori!

Soon you will be in full bloom,
The streams of Iori will water you,
And your proud cucumbers
Will embellish our tables!

Erecle turned the page. It seemed that he was
going to begin a new poem. I looked at Zurab. He
looked only half alive.

DIALOGUE WITH A PEASANT OF SAMGORI

I: Who are you, my brother,
          A man or a fable?
PEASANT: Formerly I lived in the hills
          And there I had there only a hut!
I: What are you doing now? How are you?
          Did you never become rich?
PEASANT: Of course, my brother,
          I am doing well, not badly.
          My son lives in Tiflis
          Working as a scientist.
          When I go to visit him,
          I bring him our Samgori cucumbers.

Erecle again turned a page in order to start on a
new poem, but Guram interrupted.

"Is this cycle about cucumbers or about Samgori?"
he asked.

"If he doesn't leave me alone, I'm going to sit
down," Erecle replied.

"Please, leave him alone, my dear Guram!" Zurab
said.

Guram was silent.

For a long while Erecle read poems about cucumbers, tomatoes and onions, about the cold waters of
the Iori and the trout in Tiflis lake. He even had

steamships sailing on the lake. He omitted Mephistopheles in Samgori because he could not find an appropriate rhyme. Finally he came to the end.

The audience was silent. Zurab was silent, too.

"Whose poem shall we read next?" he asked.

"Mine!" Simon Abesadze said, and he stood up.

"Come forward! Erecle, you can sit down now."

Erecle closed his notebook and looked at Zurab with frightened eyes.

"Sit down! Sit down! Your poem will be discussed next Friday," Zurab calmed him.

Erecle made his way back to us. Abesadze took his place on the platform.

"How was it?" Erecle asked Guram and me in a whisper.

"If you pour some vinegar on those poems you will get perfect pickles," Guram replied in a whisper.

Erecle angrily waved his hand and turned around. I bit my tongue to keep from laughing out loud.

"Abesadze, please begin reading!" Zurab said, and he took off his glasses.

"There is too much noise, sir!"

"Well, make them be quiet."

"The Compass," Abesadze said loudly.

As a title for a poem it was so unexpected that the whole lecture hall immediately became deathly still.

"The Compass!" Abesadze repeated.

"Which compass?" Zurab asked.

"The usual compass!" Abesadze said in amazement.

"For land, or for sea?"

"In this case, for land."

"Do you mean to say that we won't be allowed to read this poem on the sea?" Archil asked.

The hall, recently quieted, began to stir again.

"Give me a chance! It is only two verses!" Abesadze was hurt.

"Please begin!" Archil inclined his head reverently, and the poet began to read:

THE COMPASS

One needle of the compass points North,
But the other caresses the South.
Why so? What is its secret?
Why do I want to explain this idea in verse?

Why do only the North and South attract the needle?
And why does a compass always have two needles?
Because in the North there is Moscow,
And in the South there is little Gori. [1]

Abesadze finished, and smiled as proudly as though he were the inventor of the compass. The silent hall seemed stunned by his new invention. I looked at Guram. He was blinking like a man just taken from a dungeon into the sunlight. To tell the truth I, too, was completely surprised, and I waited to see how the audience would react to this poem.

"Comrades, who would like to express an opinion?" Zurab said.

Nobody spoke.

"What's the matter? Didn't you like the poem?"

"The poem is very interesting, but . . ." one of the critics began.

"Come forward, and tell us what's interesting about it," Zurab exclaimed.

"Let someone else speak first," Tserodze said.

"Say what you have to say. The others can speak later."

"I have already given my opinion. The poem is interesting. The conclusion, especially, is very well done."

"Why do you think it is very well done?" Zurab pressed the critic.

---

[1] Gori was the birthplace of Stalin.

"Well, because one needle is certainly attracted by the North, where Moscow is, and the other needle is attracted by the South, where Gori is."

"Do you think this is correct?"

"Possibly it's not correct, but it's poetic," the critic did not allow himself to be confused.

"Sit down, Tserodze. What would you say, Guram?"

"I? Nothing at all!"

"Why? Have you no opinions?"

"Of course I have opinions! But not about this poem!"

"Is the poem meaningless?"

Guram hesitated.

"The poem is not meaningless. On the contrary! The compass is seen from a very original point of view. I have never read of such a compass in any other poem."

"In general, have you ever read a poem about a compass?" Zurab persisted.

Guram opened his eyes wide, reviewed his memory, looked at us, and then shook his head in denial. "I can't remember. Probably I never have."

"Sit down! Sit down! If you remember you can tell us later," Zurab said.

Guram sat down.

"Does anybody else have an opinion?"

The hall was silent. Zurab waited for a while and then asked Abesadze: "Have you ever seen a compass, Abesadze?"

Abesadze's jaw dropped with hurt and surprise. "Are you laughing at me?"

"On the contrary. You are laughing at us. My dear fellow, you say the compass has two needles, don't you?"

Abesadze smiled ironically. "Then how many do you think it has?"

"One, Abesadze, one! It is colored at both ends. Do you understand?"

"That has no great importance in poetry."

"But it does have importance for someone who is traveling."

"I see that you have failed to grasp the main idea!" Abesadze said angrily.

"I understand Shakespeare! Is your compass more complicated than his entire works?"

Zurab smiled.

"Is it possible that you, in spite of being a candidate for a professorship, cannot understand why one needle is attracted to the North and the other to the South?" Abesadze smiled sadly.

"Why?" Zurab persisted.

"Because in the North there is Moscow, and in Moscow there is the Kremlin, and in the Kremlin there is Stalin!" Abesadze said.

"Does Stalin have a magnet in his pocket, or is there some other explanation?" Archil interrupted.

Abesadze turned purple with rage.

"Comrades!" Zurab stood up. "You can't write poems like that! In the first place, it is not necessary to write poems about compasses, opera glasses or thermometers. But if, nevertheless, you do write such poems, you should know what you are writing—about what, for what, and for whom you are writing."

"I knew very well what I was writing!" Abesadze shouted from his seat.

"What did you know, Abesadze? That a compass has two needles? What about Peking? Do we have to add a third needle? After all the Chinese invented the compass, didn't they? And what about the Persians? Aren't both Gori and Moscow North for them?"

"My poem will not be read in Persia!" Abesadze jumped up again.

"Neither will it be read in Gori, as I see the matter!" Archil said firmly.

"I am still very young," Abesadze seemed to be appealing for our sympathy and understanding.

"It is only because you are young that Archil spares you. If you weren't so young, he would probably smash that compass over your head!" Zurab said, taking Archil's side.

Laughter reigned unchecked in the hall.

"I will take my poem away and never come back to the club again!" Abesadze said in threatening tones.

"If you take your compass, not only will you never come to the club again, but you will never be able to find your way home!" Guram said.

Everyone in the hall laughed. Abesadze rushed out and slammed the door. Zurab paid no attention. When we were quiet, he sat down again.

"Well now, Baramidze, read us your poem," he smiled at me.

I felt that my poem, which was in my pocket, was burning my hand, and I hurriedly removed my hand, and then lifted it to wipe off the cold sweat.

"Comrade Zurab, I can't read anything today," I said.

"Why?" Zurab wondered.

"I haven't written anything," I lied, and my pocket began to burn again.

"Why? Why?" he repeated.

"Why should we write at all if we're only going to be criticized?" Thenguiz said.

"A poet is a pure, tender creature. You should treat him with more delicacy!" Erecle said, standing up.

"Are you delicate? Are you tender? Is Abesadze tender? If you two were yoked and harnessed, you could each plow an acre of land!"

"Our bodies are irrelevant! You should look for our souls!" one of the fledgling critics said.

"I look, but I see nothing!"

"You must search for the soul!" the critic insisted.

"I'm no Columbus! I'm only a graduate student," Zurab said, justifying himself.

"Ilya Chavchavadze discovered Barathashvili!" someone shouted.

"Barathashvili already existed before Ilya discovered him."

"You must give us time to grow!" Alavidze said.

"How much time, Alavidze? When Barathashvili was our age he was already dead!"

"On the other hand, Goethe wrote his best work, *Faust*, at the age of eighty," Alavidze commented.

"Alavidze, what on earth are you suggesting? That we sit here and wait for Erecle to be eighty years old before he writes another *Faust*?" Zurab asked.

"I'm not talking about Erecle!"

"Are you talking about Abesadze?"

"Not about Abesadze."

"Then whom are you talking about?"

"I'm talking in general terms," Alavidze gulped and sat down.

"You also wrote poems, Comrade Zurab, and, if I am not mistaken, rather bad poems?" the young critic commented.

"Yes, I wrote poems, but when I was told that they were bad, I stopped writing them," Zurab replied.

The audience began to show more interest. The hall became noisy again.

"Comrades, I am not your enemy," Zurab said, standing up. "Write good poems and I will be the first to praise you. I am the same age as you are. Who would enjoy your success more than I? Do you think I shouldn't tell Erecle that a human being, an animal, a bird, even an insect may be proud, but not a cucumber? No one should write poems about cucumbers. What if someday an American poet were to write a poem saying 'The needle of the compass points North and South, because Truman is in the North and Chiang Kai-shek is in the South'? Unfortunately, every country has a North and a South. You must know that our literary circle is not destined to produce forty geniuses. God forbid that forty Barathashvilis and Ilya Chavchavadzes should be found in one university! Don't deceive yourselves. Georgia will be lucky if, out of this group, there emerge one or two talented poets, or novelists, or

critics, or translators. If we don't realize this and
don't believe it, it's better to get up right now, put
on our hats and go home."

Zurab stopped speaking. The audience was spellbound, and nobody moved. Forty men sat and listened
to this man who for years had been silent in the last
row. He had never said anything—neither good nor
bad. But now there was a strange gleam in his eyes,
and in a voice trembling with sincerity he was telling
us truths that we had never heard before.

The meeting was over, but none of us dared to be
the first to stand up and leave. Zurab sensed our embarrassment, so he was the first to turn and leave.
"Remember, I always told you he was a man with
guts," Guram said, and went out.

Okropeta's Tavern

Okropeta's tavern is in Navthluhi, in a place so dirty that a decent man would have trouble finding it. Okropeta is like an independent state. In his tavern there is always lamb, fillet of beef, salted meat, boiled pork, pickles, long white loaves of bread, Thushethi cheese, three-year-old wine, and many other kinds of food—all for extraordinarily high prices. To have a good time at Okropeta's you must pawn or mortgage everything you own. But the taste and memory of his excellent food will remain with you to the grave. Everyone who wants to avoid displaying his riches ostentatiously in the public restaurants goes to Okropeta, eats, drinks, revels, listens to sentimental songs, and in a softhearted moment sticks a hundred-ruble note on the forehead of the one-eyed musician, Orshaura. Okropeta knows his clients: he knows how to take care of them, and how to speak with each one of them.

When Okropeta saw us, he put one hand on his hip and with the other plunged an enormous knife into the counter, saying loudly: "I don't accept watches, passports or coats as deposit!"

"Greetings, Uncle Okropeta!" Guram smiled at him, and raised his hand like a German general.

"I don't take student certificates either!" Okropeta said, glaring at us.

"Today is scholarship day, Uncle Okropeta!" Guram said, and he put his hand into his pocket.

"What's the date, today?" Okropeta asked us, still dubious.

"The twenty-fifth," I said.

"Sit down!" said Okropeta, a bit mollified.

"What's the matter? I don't see any customers here?" Guram gave Okropeta a gentle punch on the shoulder.

"It's early," Okropeta said.

Guram and I sat down at a table. Okropeta left the counter and leaned on our table with his huge paws.

"What do you want to order?" he asked.

"What do you have?" I asked in turn.

"The tavern of Okropeta is like a wishing stone in a fairy tale! Make a wish!" he said. I did. And within ten minutes there appeared on our table two loaves of bread, some Thushethi cheese, two fillets, pickles, cucumbers, tomatoes and four bottles of wine.

"Where is he?" Okropeta asked me.

"Who?"

"The one who has a big head and usually reads very long and eccentric poems."

"There are a lot of people like that!" I said I could not remember any special person.

"He has a high-pitched voice, tries to make it deeper, and at the end of the evening hits himself on the head with a bottle," Okropeta went on.

"Oh, him! He was killed today. We're going to bury him next Friday!" I said, remembering Erecle.

I poured out some wine.

"I knew he'd be killed someday! He was very bad when he was drunk," Okropeta had some pity. "How was he killed?"

"How was he killed?" I asked Guram.

"Whom are you talking about?" Guram asked me in astonishment.

"About Erecle."

"Oh, he wasn't the only one! Another one was killed, too," Guram said, pointing at me. "They wanted to kill him, but he was saved."

"How's that? They would have killed him?" Okropeta became angry.

"Sure! And for no reason!"

"Whom do you mean?"

"One man!"

"Probably you committed some crime!" Okropeta said, and returned to the counter.

"Nothing important. I only wrote bad poems."

"Well, what does it matter to him?" Okropeta was surprised again.

"This man affirms that bad poems are lethal," I said.

"And you couldn't tell him that a book is not a bullet, and if you don't like it you can close it!"

"I told him that."

"Well?"

"He doesn't believe it."

"Let him read, then. It will serve him right!" Okropeta waved his hand. "You mean he killed two men?" he repeated.

"He didn't really kill them, but if they had any consciences, they would commit suicide," Guram said.

"Couldn't you say that in the beginning? My heart was nearly broken!" Okropeta said. From the half-opened door a beardless soldier asked in Russian, *"Borshch yest?"*

"Where would I get borshch from?" the astonished Okropeta asked me.

"*Chevo?*" the soldier did not understand Georgian.

"*Nyetu,*" snapped Okropeta, and the head disappeared.

Silence fell in the tavern. Only the rustle of a broom could be heard, and the tinkling of plates. The wall in front of me was painted with hunting scenes. In one picture a fleeing deer had its rump pierced by an arrow. While waiting for the next arrow, he looked at the hunter with strangely sad eyes. The hunter was aiming a rifle at him. Beside that, hunting dogs with bared teeth snarled at a wild boar, and piglets cowered behind a big pig and awaited their fate. The third picture presented an example of philanthropic, humane and compassionate action, for the hunter was killing a fox who held a terrorstricken rooster in his mouth.

This interesting picture gallery ended with an even more interesting notice written, for some reason, in Russian instead of Georgian, which warned the customers: "Singing, Making Noise, and Dancing are Strictly Prohibited."

"Singing, making noise, and dancing are strictly prohibited," hummed Guram, and he filled the glasses.

We drank the first bottle in silence. We only touched glasses. With the second bottle, Guram was visited by the speech-making muse. He filled the glasses, coughed and prepared to speak.

"But I want to speak!" he said.

"You don't really want to," I said.

"Yes, I do," he replied, "then go ahead."

Guram went ahead. "How many years have I known you?" he asked me.

"Many," I said, a little surprised.

"Well, how many?"

"One, two, three . . . You've known me from the kindergarten!"

"So?"

"What do you mean by 'so'?"

"How long have you known me?"

"If you are my friend, drink! Don't sit there goggling at me!" I said.

"I am already drunk. Long live our friendship!" Guram said, and tipped the glass to his mouth.

"Long life!" I said, and drank.

Guram filled the glasses again.

"Now I want to drink to the health of your mother," he said.

I lifted my head. Guram was slowly and carefully taking a piece of cork out of his glass with his little finger. Probably he was thinking of how to make the toast.

"Not only to your mother, but to mothers in general—your mother first."

"Why my mother?"

"Because!"

"I thank you," I said, and raised my glass.

"Wait! Don't drink yet!" Guram stopped me.

I put the glass down on the table.

"I want to drink a toast to God!"

"But you wanted to drink to the health of my mother!"

"I wish to drink a toast to God—God in disgrace, fallen into disrepute, the lost God, the forgotten God, the humiliated God."

"Long live the discredited and deceived God!" I said.

"You are a fool," Guram said.

"What about you?" I asked.

"I'm a fool, too, for drinking wine with you. I am a bigger fool than you because I am with you, and I propose a toast to God!"

"What are you waiting for, my dear? Why are you nagging me?"

"I want to drink a toast to God!"

"Drink then! Who's stopping you?"

"Stand up!" I stood. "Long live your mother."

"Thank you."

"Do you know who your mother is?" Guram asked me.

I had no answer. Guram looked at me for a long time, a very long time, then poured some wine in his glass and began:

"Your mother is God. That you sit and look at her, and she sits and looks at you, that you call her Mother and she calls you son. Do you think there is no God? Who do you think God is? A bearded grandfather who sits on a cloud and washes His face and makes the rain? God is so clear, so near, so obvious and so simple that when you see Him, you don't know that He is God, you cannot imagine that He is God, you cannot believe that He is God. That is God's misfortune. That's why people have no faith in God. If God were somewhere else, far from us, alone and on high, if God were not among us, then everyone would believe in Him. That is the absolute truth! You must believe in God even though He has no face. When He is there, when He does not say He is God, when He breaks bread with you, prepares your dinner, dresses you, covers your head, smiles at you and caresses you, kisses you, weeps because of you, is cold, thirsty and hungry with you, dies for you, gives His soul to the devil for your sake—then you must believe in such a God. But when God shows you His face, stands you in the corner, pulls your ears, and says to you: 'I am God, believe in Me,' then why should He need your faith? Not only you, but everyone will accept such a God. You must believe in God when He is like you, like me, like your mother. Do you understand?" Guram finished and peered at me with misty eyes.

"I understand," I said, and to put an end to his harangue I drank some wine.

"*Bon appétit!*" Guram said, and sat down. Okropeta brought two more bottles and looked pointedly at Guram as though to say, "What's the matter with him?"

"He is ashamed to face you," I said.

Guram poured wine for Okropeta. "Let's drink to the health of Teymo's mother!"

Okropeta wiped his fat lips on the tablecloth and reached for a glass. "I will just take a sip," he said.

"Drain the glass," Guram insisted.

"My life for your mother's lives," Okropeta said.

"Drink!"

"My life for the breasts of your mother, who raised such a good young man," continued Okropeta.

"Drink!" Guram encouraged him.

"To your mother's—"

"Drink, my friend, and stop bothering us . . ." I said to Okropeta.

Okropeta drank, then he looked sideways at me and took back one of the bottles he had brought.

"Where are you taking it?" Guram asked.

"One is enough for you," Okropeta said.

"Do you think one is enough?" Guram asked me. I nodded.

"Pour the wine!"

I poured the wine. Guram took his glass.

"To your health, Teymuri!" he said.

"To our health together!" I replied.

"Good! To yours and mine, Teymuri. I love you very much, and do you know why?"

"Yes, I know."

"You don't know anything! Why, then?"

"All right, I don't know."

"That's what I thought. Well, this is why. You are my brother, my real brother. At first I was afraid of you, then ashamed of you. For a long time I was both afraid and ashamed of you."

"What were you afraid of?"

"I don't know. I was afraid because you were completely alone."

"Why?"

"I don't know. When something was lost in class, I was afraid you had taken it. When you missed a class, I was afraid that you wouldn't return to school. When Thavera was caught stealing, I was afraid they would arrest you too. When we finished high school, I was afraid you wouldn't go on to the university. Then, when all my fears proved unfounded, I was ashamed and glad at the same time."

Guram fell silent for a while, and then he said: "So you and I are brothers?"

"Of course. What about it?"

"Remember this: if anything happens to you, I shall commit suicide."

"I've always said you're crazy."

"Even so!" he took his glass and drank.

I wanted to make a toast, so I stood up. "Long live you and me, Guram! Long live what you call God! Long live man, tall, strong, just and good. Long live faith and the loss of faith. I will now go home and burn all the poems I have ever written. I will burn everything."

"You will have the thanks of a grateful posterity," Guram smiled.

"I will burn everything. Then I will sit until morning and read a poem written by God—a poem by this God who is so simple, so light, so near that you can't even believe He is God:

> I have held a harp to my breast:
> As I have desired it,
> The splendid beams
> Have shone for me.
> He built firm
> Who built it,
> And adorned with sky
> The great Nikortsmenda . . .

"Long live God, Guram—your God and mine! The God who is not sitting on a cloud washing His face, or making rain . . . who for our sake gives His soul to the devil."

I emptied the glass and sat down. Then I closed my eyes and swam in a blue and rose-colored sea of stars. I felt an enormous paw on my shoulder and opened my eyes. I saw him swimming in the mist, and he was no God, he was the devil. He held in his hand the abacus and he had come to take my soul and Guram's away from us.

When I entered the room, my mother was sitting at the window reading. The door was open, so she did not notice my arrival. She read with assurance, frowning attentively. During all this time I had never told her about my poems, and she had never asked me. However I felt that she guessed something, because during the night when I was writing my poems I often felt her eyes on me. How many times did I get up, come to her, bend over her face and know that under the trembling eyelids two curious and amazed eyes were looking at me! Then I could write no more and I would close the notebook and go to bed.

I saw that my notebook was lying in my mother's hands. An unpleasant shiver—perhaps of fear—ran through my body. She was absorbed in reading. I stood close beside her.

"Mother!"

My mother jumped, closed the notebook and looked up at me, a little frightened. Then she blushed.

"This notebook, son . . ." Speech failed her. "Don't be hurt. I will only read it and then put it back in its place again." She looked at me yearningly. I was at a loss. "Of course, Mother. I didn't show it to you simply because I thought you wouldn't like it."

"There's not much more to read—only one or two poems," my mother said, and she opened the notebook.

I went to the kitchen to give her time to finish reading. When I returned, she had put down the book and was setting the table.

"Did you like the poems, my mother?" I said with artificial calm, as I sat down at the table. My mother smiled and nodded her head.

"What do you think of them?" I was interested, and my heart was beating fast.

"They aren't bad," my mother said quietly, and she began to cut the bread.

"What do you mean, 'not bad'?" I said, frightened.

"Do *you* like them?" my mother asked me.

My mouth went dry and I swallowed saliva. "Of course I like them. That's why I write them . . . that is . . . well . . . well, in general, everyone likes his own work."

"Well, son, you see, I prepared dinner for today. I spent a long time at it, and now I don't like it," my mother said.

"When I don't like a poem, I tear it up and throw it away."

"I, nevertheless, waited for you. I thought, 'Maybe Teymuri will like it.' Now taste it," my mother said.

I tasted the bean sauce with little enthusiasm. I don't know—did it just seem to me, or was it really, strangely tasteless? I set the plate aside.

"Now you see, you are left hungry," my mother said, and with a sad face she sat down at the table.

"But what is wrong with my poems?"

"Nothing, son. Nothing is wrong. Everything is in its own place—rhyme, rhythm, syllable, periods, commas . . ."

"Then what more do you want?" I insisted.

My mother put both hands to her head and closed her eyes. She sat that way for a long time and finally she said:

"A poem is like a man, son. How many people have hands, feet, eyes, ears, nose, everything in its right place? We think they are human beings, but when we get to know them, we come to the conclusion that they are not human beings. The more we look at them, and hear them, the more we are convinced they are not real human beings, that they lack something, and this lack, this defect, makes them not humans but animals, beasts. Don't be hurt, my son, but your poems lack something—something which cannot be written, and cannot be seen on paper."

"Do you mean to say my poems lack soul?"

"No, son, how can I say that soul is lacking? On the contrary, there is too much soul—so much that there is no room for your own soul."

"I don't understand what you're saying!"

"That you don't understand is the whole point!"

"You don't like anything I do! You don't believe in anything! I will never be able to do anything you will like!" I became angry.

"No, son. Where do you get such ideas? If you write my death sentence—even that would be precious to me. But your soul, your blood, your sweat and pain must be in it. You must write about things that pain you."

"Then what about this?" I shouted and grabbed the notebook.

"It is nothing, son. It is simply exercises. You are a talented young man, you make very pleasant rhymes, nothing more," my mother said, and she began to tidy up the plates.

I had never before seen my mother so direct, so open, so severe toward me, and I was a little frightened. My mother felt she had treated me very harshly, and I saw compassion in her eyes. She arranged the plates clumsily. First a glass tumbled down, then a spoon fell from her hand and finally she broke a plate. I came up to her and put my arm around her shoulder.

"Do you think I am hurt?" I said and smiled at her.

"No, son. I was probably in a bad humor. Really, you have many pretty poems. Especially the one which was probably written about Gulika—'Give me your smile as a gift,' or the other one, 'The moonlight fell like flint and steel,' or 'I left a little house in the country.' These I liked very, very much. I'm sure that Gulika also likes your poems. Today I just got out of bed on the wrong side. I myself don't know what happened to me. I read them with such pleasure, and then all of a sudden—I really don't know, as God is my witness."

My mother was excited, confused, trembling.

"Really I liked them! In one place I even cried. Which poem was it? Yes, the one you wrote about me—I liked it very, very much . . ."

She lied terribly, without taking her eyes off me. She forgot everything she had told me only a few minutes before and placed all the blame on herself, for fear of losing me again and becoming once again a stranger to me. The more troubled she became, the more she talked and lied, the closer, the more beloved, the dearer she was to me. Something clutched at my throat; I wanted to snatch the green notebook from my mother's hand—to tear it and burn it—and then to embrace her, to kiss her trembling hands. But I did not dare, and I went out of the room.

The Sea

———

The sand is hot. I have covered my eyes with Gulika's scarf, and I am looking through it at the sun. The sun is many-colored like Gulika's scarf: red, green, black, yellow, lilac and some other color which is a mixture of those in addition to the sun's own color. I narrow my eyelid with a finger, and now, spread out like the fan of a peacock's tail, the beautiful sun trembles in the sky. I narrow the other eyelid, and then the sky seems to be embroidered with innumerable beautiful suns lying one above the other. Probably Eskimos always see that kind of a sky—a sky full of suns and colors. What happiness, God!

I laugh at my own naive thoughts and I take my

hands from my eyelids. Once again a single sun looks at me from the sky.

"Fifteen minutes have passed. You should turn over now!" the beach attendant warned us. Nobody counts time on the beach at Batum except the Russians. For this reason, they have a moderate, pleasant suntan. We Georgians are terribly sunburnt.

Suddenly a shadow fell on my face. I pulled down the scarf and looked up at the shadow. A woman with a marble-white face, large blue eyes, black hair, stood by my head. I squinted involuntarily and smiled at her. She was the same woman who had come to my room yesterday evening, asking about someone named Afto.

"Excuse me. You and Afto are sharing this room, aren't you?" she had said.

"Afto who?"

"Afto!"

"Of course! Please sit down."

"Your name is Guivi, isn't it?"

"Yes." God, how pretty she is! . . . "Please sit down!"

"Where is Afto?"

"Afto?" . . . What beautiful eyes she has! What black hair!

"Will Afto come back soon?" she asked.

"Yes, very soon. Please sit down."

The girl sat and began to look around the room.

"May I offer you a glass of champagne?" I held up the bottle.

"No, thank you."

"A lemonade?"

"No!"

"Some chocolate, perhaps?"

"Where is Afto? He promised to meet me at the station. Probably he was very busy. He promised to get me a room, too! It's only by luck that I got a room. I left Tiflis a day after Afto. You did arrive together, didn't you?"

"Who? Afto and I? Yes, we arrived together."

"I'm in room 105, downstairs. Please tell him to ring me when he comes," she said, and stood up.

"I tell you what! Please sit down, sit down for a little while. Let's drink one glass of champagne to our acquaintance."

"Good!" the girl smiled, and took a glass. I took one, too, and we clinked our glasses.

"To our acquaintance!"

"So be it!" she said.

We smiled at each other; suddenly the smile died on my face. I turned pale. The astonished woman first looked at me, and then followed my fixed gaze. At the door stood Gulika, red with anger, petrified and mortified. Everything was like a scene from a cheap operetta. Gulika slammed the door and the surprised girl put down her glass.

"What has happened?" she asked me.

"Nothing much . . ." I said and dashed out of the room. I ran to Gulika's door. It was locked from the inside. When I returned to my room, a surprised Guram was sitting on the bed, scratching his head. The girl was nowhere to be seen.

"What happened?" Guram said.

"Did she say anything?"

"She said, 'When is Afto coming?'"

"And then?"

"I said he is not coming. Why? she asked me, and I said because in the first place I don't know who Afto is, and in the second place, Afto doesn't live here."

"And what then?"

"Then nothing. Idiot! she shouted in Russian and left . . . I don't know why she insulted me."

"I'm lost. Gulika saw us together."

"What were you doing?"

"We were drinking champagne."

"And afterward?"

"Nothing."

"Who is she?"

"I don't know."

"Enough! Who is ever going to swallow that!" Guram laughed and lay back on the bed.

Once, so the story goes, two friends, who had not seen each other for a long time, met. One man was sad and the other was cheerful.

"How are you?" the cheerful one said.

"A strange and unfortunate thing has happened to me! But nobody will believe me. Why should I believe you will believe me?" the other answered, sighing.

"What terrible thing has happened to make you so miserable?" the cheerful one asked with a feeling of pity.

"My wife turned me out of the house."

"Why?"

"This is the reason," the sad man said, and he began to tell him the whole story.

"A month ago I was on my way home. It was a cold, rainy day. Suddenly I heard a squeaky voice in front of me. I bent down and saw a frog, an ordinary frog. 'Pick me up, my good man. You can see that I am dying from cold!' the frog said. So I picked up the frog, put it inside my coat and brought it home. I put it on the windowsill and started to eat my supper. 'Give me something to eat, my good man!' the frog said. What could I do? I put it on the table and gave it some food. I don't remember if it also drank something or not. Then I went to bed, and once more I heard the voice of the frog: 'I'm afraid to be alone, my good friend. Take me to your bed!' What would you have done in my place? I picked it up and took it to bed with me. The frog pressed close to me, and miracle! it turned into a beautiful woman. Just at that moment my wife entered the room. When she saw us, she lost her senses and fainted. As soon as she regained consciousness I told her the whole story in detail, but she didn't believe me, and drove me out of the house."

"Who would believe you, poor fellow! Such a story!" the happy man said.

"Didn't I tell you that you wouldn't believe me," the unhappy man said, and went on his way even more mournful than before.

I did not know whether Gulika believed what I told her. But now, clear as day, that same girl was standing by my head.

"Excuse me, is this chair free?" she asked, and touched Gulika's beach chair with her pretty foot.

"Please sit down!" I said, and moved Gulika's shoes toward me.

"Is it free?" she repeated. I felt that behind her glasses, her eyes were on Gulika's shoes.

"Yes, it's free," I said, and stood up.

The girl bowed, and put her hand on the chair. In my heart I thought—She will straighten it and sit down; and I was glad. Instead she took one end of the chair and dragged it away. I was baffled. She walked away without looking back.

"Excuse me, young lady!" I said.

"Did you say something to me?" she turned to me.

"Well, really . . ." I wanted to tell her that the beach chair was taken, that I thought she would sit with me and . . . but I couldn't say any of that, so I stammered awkwardly, "Are you from Tiflis?"

"Yes, what about it?" she asked and took off her glasses.

"Oh, that's why you are very white," I smiled at her.

"Never mind. I will get darker," she reassured me.

"For the love of God, don't do that!" I said.

"I will do what you wish," she said comfortingly.

"I thank you," I said, and bowed my head in gratitude.

"Not at all!" she answered, and then she put her glasses on again, and continued on her way. She stopped ten meters away, put the chair down skillfully, and began to take off her skirt. When she had the skirt over her head and arms she looked at my direction. I avoided her eyes and gazed out at the sea.

The sea was calm, so calm that you could hear even the slight noise of the waves.

The sea was rustling and whispering. The shore was roaring, and the sand was tinkling and jingling. Languid people with half-closed eyes were strewn under the burning sun. Some, bathed in sweat, played cards, while others played football, spoke loudly, laughed, roared with laughter. Some, with faces in the sand, turned over their arms and exposed their still untanned underarms to the sun. The majority plunged into the sea, as self-indulgently as though the sea were full of absolute love for everything and everybody. Some went far, far out into the sea, where the water was blue, completely blue, and their heads appeared now and then like little islands and then disappeared again. From far away you could hear the shouting of these islands, their laughter, false alarms screaming and yelling which the sea breeze carried to the shore as it carried the low whispering of the waves. It was as if the sea were talking to itself in a thousand different tongues. And these people, who had flocked here from all the corners of the earth, who were now lying on the bosom of the sea and were sighing with pleasure, moaning, laughing, keeping silence, did not exist for the sea. The sea was very quiet.

The girl took off her dress and put on a cherry-red bathing suit. To my surprise, her body was not as white as her face. It was more like the color of wheat, and all these colors together—the white, black, red and wheat—produced a wonderful effect. She probably

uses makeup on her face, I thought, and then I got up.
The girl lay back in the chair.

Suddenly a tall, handsome, broad-shouldered, short-
haired young man came up and stood unceremoni-
ously above her.

"What did he want?" he asked the girl. I heard
this and my heart contracted.

"Who?" the girl asked.

"That character!" the young man said, glancing in
my direction. Obviously he didn't care if I heard or
not. My hands turned cold, but I tried to look as if
I hadn't heard anything. I bent down, picked up a
pebble and threw it into the sea. The pebble skipped
across the surface of the water.

"Him? Nothing!"

"He talked to you about something!"

"Nothing!" said the girl, taking off her glasses. "I
asked for the beach chair, and he gave it to me."

"Nothing else?"

"Nothing else!"

"He smiled at you?"

"He did not smile at me!" the girl said, and put
her glasses on again.

"Well"—the conversation continued in low voices.
I don't know what they were talking about, but the
young man laughed loudly, then knelt at her side,
squeezed her elbows with both his hands, and laid
his head on hers. I looked out to sea again.

"Teymo! Teymo!" Guram waved at me. He and
Gulika swam toward the shore. I waved at them,
and lay on the sand, face upward.

I like the sea very much, but I never swim far out
with the others. Only when I'm alone do I go far,
sometimes so far that I can no longer see the shore.
Then I am very frightened of the sea, because it is
so enormous—a million, billion times greater than I—
and it can destroy me, swallow me, smash me within
its quiet and heavy grasp, without noticing, or under-

standing, or feeling anything. But at the same time I am not afraid, because the sea has a wonderfully soft body and is remarkably warm. If the sea accepts you, it will never drown you. The sea is not treacherous, but it does not like not to be feared. It warns you itself, tells you, begs, roars, presses down on the land with its huge breakers the size of a house. It gives you a push to keep you from coming too near, but if you still dare, the sea does not like you to be fearless. The sea has a sea-size pride, the sea is a living thing, and when it talks, everyone must listen.

One, two, three, four . . . The sun is four fingers' width above the horizon: the sun itself is three fingers wide—altogether seven fingers. Therefore the sunset should take place in two hours.

Where are they? Couldn't they reach the shore?

Guram was the first to come out of the water. Panting, he ran up to me and began to leap around on one leg, sprinkling me with drops of water.

"Please, shake yourself a bit farther off!" I said.

"Did you see how far we were?" he said, and dug his blue chin into the sand.

"Where?" I asked.

"Far!"

"What did you see?"

"What should we have seen?" Guram asked in astonishment.

Gulika reached the shore. Now she began to skip and jump around me.

"The towel, please!" Gulika said.

"Here!" I threw her the towel.

Gulika dried herself, then looked around, surprised. I looked away.

"Where is the beach chair?"

"What?" I pretended innocence.

"The chair!" she repeated.

"Ah, the chair! Where is the chair?" I asked Guram.

"Which chair?" Guram was more astonished than I.

"My chair!" Gulika said, and frowned.

"Gulika's chair was here!" Guram agreed.

"Some scientists affirm that objects can move by themselves."

"Get up and bring the chair here immediately!" Gulika said to me.

I looked around. The girl and the young man were in the sea, but their clothes were lying on the chair.

"Get up, Guram, and get the chair. It's standing over there!" I said to Guram.

"Since you were the one who gave it away, you can bring it back," Guram said, and closed his eyes.

The woman came out of the water and went toward the chair. Gulika looked first at the woman and then at me.

"You gave it to her?" she asked suddenly.

I did not answer.

"Why did you give it to her?" Gulika said.

"I don't know!" I answered, and looked straight into her eyes.

"Who is she?"

"I don't know!"

"You don't know?"

"No!"

I looked toward the girl. She was watching us. She probably guessed what we were talking about. Suddenly she got up, grabbed the chair and pulled it in our direction. I didn't know where to go.

"I beg your pardon. I took it without permission," she said, as she approached us. She put the chair back in its place.

"Not at all. We don't need it," Gulika said, rather coldly.

"We don't need it either," the girl smiled at Gulika.

"All the more reason!" Gulika said.

"What do you mean—all the more reason?" the girl asked in surprise.

"Nothing! Take it, we don't need it anymore!"

"Neither do we!"

"Then you can take it back to the rental office. Only remember to return my certificate to me. I left my student certificate there. My name is Gulika, last name Tchibadze."

"Gulika!" I entreated.

"Turn round!" Gulika said. I turned, and when I turned back again, there was neither the girl, nor the chair, nor Gulika. Gulika, having put on her dress, was leaving the beach.

"I'm going too," Guram said, and picked up his trousers.

"Stay here and look at the sunset," I begged him.

"I can't let Gulika go alone."

"Wait!"

"You surprise me! You are an absolute idiot!" Guram said, and sat down.

I looked in the direction of the girl. The tall young man had put the chair under his arm and was carrying it back to the beach house. The woman was putting on her dress. I did not avert my eyes. She was like a very pretty statue with her raised arm and half-bent knee. When she put on the skirt and checked how it clung to her thighs, she looked in my direction and smiled to me.

"Maybe you are not an idiot after all," Guram sighed.

There was only three fingers' width to go till sunset. Soon the sun touched the sea, and a golden sparkling path stretched from the far horizon to the shore. I wanted to jump up and run along this path—run fast, fast—so that I could reach the sun and touch it before it set. I wanted this so much that I even stood up. Guram sat thoughtfully looking at the sun.

The sun was already half inside the sea. The golden path narrowed, grew dimmer, stretching like a cable between the sun and shore. Guram suddenly jumped up and ran like a madman toward the boulevard. In amazement I followed him with my eyes.

He ran, taking big steps, tripping in the sand, falling down, standing again, and running on, away from the beach. In a minute he was back, still running like a madman. He rushed to the shore and laid a huge, blue hydrangea on the path of the sun. Then he turned and sat down beside me, panting.

"I offered a flower to the sun!" he said, and smiled at me with a happy face.

I did not answer, only nodded and smiled at him. At the same time I felt envy, a great envy, a real envy, that it was not I who had thought of making an offering. Only the edge of the sun could be seen now. The beam was like a golden hand stretched out from the end of the sea. A huge, blue hydrangea rested on the palm of the hand.

The sun set. The path, and the flower, disappeared in the dusk.

"Did you see it, Guram? The sun accepted the flower!" I said.

Guram smiled again. The sun had accepted his flower, his offering.

All the armchairs in the lobby of the Intourist Hotel were occupied. Gulika was nowhere to be seen. I did not want to go up to her room.

"Come down to the café!" I said to Guram, and hung the towel on his shoulder.

"And Gulika?" Guram asked.

"I'll call her!"

"It would be better if you went up to see her."

"I'll telephone!"

I went to the manager's desk, and picked up a telephone.

"Welcome, Teymuri!" the manager greeted me.

"Long life, Sasha!"

"I have to transfer you to another room. Some foreigners have arrived."

"Why do you always bother me? Am I some kind of prize cup that is awarded to each room in turn?"

"What can I do? It is an order from above!" Sasha shrugged.

"What do you mean, 'from above'?" The manager looked up somewhere in the direction to God, and blinked his eyes.

"Couldn't you say there is already someone in the room?"

"It wouldn't help."

"If it doesn't help, then I just won't leave my room!"

"They would force you to leave!"

"Who?"

"They!"

"Who are they?"

"Leave me alone. I have enough troubles. I tell you I'll give you another room!"

"Hello, room 302, please," I asked the operator.

"Three-oh-two doesn't answer," the operator said. I hung up.

"When are you going to transfer me?" I asked the manager.

"You have already been transferred to 303," he said without raising his head.

"Have you written any new poems?" I asked him.

"I wrote one last night. May I read it to you?"

"Tomorrow. I have no time now."

Gulika was sitting before the mirror, combing her hair.

"It is customary to knock before entering," she said.

I went back out, knocked, and came in again.

"Please sit down," Gulika said.

I sat on the bed. Gulika continued combing her hair. She spread out the golden hair until it looked like the sun which had recently accepted the flower.

"Aren't you ashamed, child? Why are you angry with me?" I said.

"Of course I'm ashamed! Can't you see—even my hair is turning red with shame!"

"Let's go down for some coffee."

"You go. I'll come later."

"I've been transferred to the room next to yours. Some foreigners are arriving."

"Fine."

"One more delegation, and I'll be moving in with you."

"Poor boy! How sorry I am for you!" Gulika shook her head in pity.

"Get up and let's go down together!"

"You go down, and I'll come later."

"No, let's go together!"

"I have to change my dress!"

"Put on the blue dress."

"It's no business of yours what I put on!"

"All right, I'll go," I said.

Guram was in the café. He was saving a place for us. He was reading the newspaper. I sat down in the chair near a window.

"Where were you? My stomach is nearly dry. Gulika isn't coming?"

"She is coming. Have you ordered anything?"

"Why should I order? The waiter knows what to bring," Guram said, and went on reading.

The waiter brought three coffees, three sandwiches, and a bottle of mineral water.

"How much does this sausage cost?" Guram looked suspiciously at the sandwich.

"Don't be afraid. The bill won't be more than five rubles," the waiter calmed him.

"What do I have to be afraid of? You're the one who has to be afraid!"

"If you have no money, why didn't you stay in Tiflis? What's so wonderful about Batum that you starve yourselves for a whole month? Are you out of a job? Your misery nearly kills me!" The waiter's heart was overcome with pity.

"It's not wise to eat so much before going to sleep!" Guram informed him.

"And morning and noon, too?"

"Go, my dear! Mind your own business! Don't worry about our dying of hunger!" Guram was offended.

"I have a certain amount of sympathy for the girl, but as for you, you can starve for all I care," the waiter said, and went away.

The café was full of the pleasant smell of tobacco and Turkish coffee. The window was open and a breeze came in. There were many people about. A short distance away Dursun sits at a table. There were already ten little coffee cups, all empty and turned over, in front of him. He was drinking his eleventh cup. From time to time he stared fixedly into it, then put it down, and taking up another cup, he would look fixedly at the coffee grounds at the bottom. Thus he examined and reexamined all of them, shaking his head in dissatisfaction, and he continued to drink the coffee. Dursun is probably fifty-five or sixty years old—it is difficult to say, exactly. He sat in the same place last year, and the year before last, and three years ago, and even longer ago than that. He always drank coffee, and always looked for something in the sediment at the bottom of the cups.

They say that Dursun knows how to read tea leaves and coffee grounds. He sees strange things: misfortune, happiness, love, hate, money, riches, women, death, journeys, short and sharp, long and hazardous. He sees paths which are united somewhere on the side of the cup, and these paths branch off only to join together later; they grow shorter and longer; they separate, rejoin, lengthen out again, and so on, without end and without hope.

So he sits there and tells fortunes for everyone who wants to hear them, predicts life's pathways for everyone. There he sits at a table in the corner. In the bottom of innumerable cups he has read the future of innumerable people.

Is it possible that he never saw his own future?

For some unknown reason, his future ended in this café.

The short-haired young man and another young fellow entered the café. They sat down near us and leaned a chair against their table.

"They are probably waiting for the girl," I thought.

The waiter came up to them. "I suppose you are only going to order coffee and mineral water, like the others," he said, looking in our direction.

"Three plates of roast chicken, one cognac, two mineral water, a bottle of champagne, three bottles of lemonade and six coffees," the short-haired one said.

"God bless you!" the waiter said happily.

"What have you got for dessert?" the young man asked.

"Pickles!" the waiter smiled.

"Oh, you are a great one!" the man laughed, and slapped him on the shoulder.

The waiter left.

"This bitch has cost me a fortune! Ten days we spent in Gagri!" the short-haired man said to the bulging-eyed fellow, and with an air of hurt pride he moved the ashtray around on the table.

"What kind of agreement do you have with her?" the bulging-eyed fellow asked.

"What can I possibly have? She just attached herself to me. Last year, Jemal had her in Sochi."

"Leave her, and put an end to it!"

"I can't leave her now."

"Do you love her?" the bulging-eyed man asked with a wry grimace.

I heard everything. Strangely I could feel my whole body shivering with cold.

"Did you love her?" the bulging-eyed man repeated. The waiter brought their order and put it on the table.

"Not in the least! But she has a nice body," the short-haired one smiled.

"Couldn't you find a better bitch than her at the

seaside? If I had your money, I would get a real angel!" the bulging-eyed fellow said.

"Stop talking, she is coming. Lia, come here!" short-hair called and waved his hand.

She entered the café. She was so beautiful that Guram covered his face with his hands, kept them there for a while and finally removed his hands from his eyes, looked at her and sighed.

"Ah!"

"Shut up!" I warned him.

I looked at Lia. She smiled at me again.

Suddenly the doors opened, and Guram and I dropped our jaws in surprise. In the doorway stood Gulika, her head held high like a gazelle's. Her hair was hanging down to her shoulders, she wore enormously high heels and a scarlet dress, which was décolleté down to the navel. She came toward us with a proud expression and a subtle swaying of her body. The whole café turned and looked at her. Involuntarily I stood up and gave her my place. Guram swallowed his coffee like wine and began to cough. Gulika sat down, took a cigarette from her red handbag and exhaled a great cloud of smoke.

"Are you crazy, woman?" I said.

"What's the matter?" Gulika was astonished.

"What do you look like!"

"What do I look like, Guram?" Gulika asked, blowing smoke into Guram's face.

"If you were attached to a pole you could be a red flag!" Guram said, and looked at me.

"Really?" Gulika turned to me.

"Go upstairs and change at once!" I said.

"Why, my darling? You like this kind of a woman, don't you? Waiter!" Gulika shouted. The waiter trotted over at once. "At your disposal, ma'am."

"One bottle of cognac, one bottle of champagne, three plates of roast chicken!"

"And one doctor and one policeman for me! I can't pay for that," Guram exploded.

The waiter hesitated.

"Bring what I told you!" Gulika said, and the waiter went away.

"What happened to you, Gulika?" I said in a low voice, furtively gazing at the neighboring table.

Lia lifted her champagne glass up to her eyes and smiled at us from behind the glass.

"If I am disturbing you, I shall leave," Gulika said, and put out her cigarette.

I relaxed a little. "Please stay, but just don't behave so provocatively!" I said.

"Am I doing anything wrong, Guram?" she turned to Guram.

"On the contrary! You make everything rosy!" he said.

The waiter brought us the cognac and grilled chicken.

Gulika poured out the cognac, and began pronouncing a toast: "Victory to all beautiful women, all lovely and passionate women!"

She touched her glass to mine, and drank. I drank without a word. I wanted to fall through the floor.

"Long live Gulika!" Guram said.

"No! Long live beautiful women!" Gulika corrected him. She poured the cognac again.

"My dear Gulika! Do you know how much this cognac costs?" Guram said. He turned the bottle around.

"One million!"

"Bring it down a little."

"Half a million!"

"Exactly!"

"So what?"

"Where will you get this half a million?"

"Teymuri will pay!"

The glass fell out of my hand. Guram swallowed his cognac the wrong way and began to hiccough.

"Fill the glasses!" Gulika commanded, and Guram filled them.

The short-haired young man got up from the neighboring table and came to us.

Gulika gave him a surprised look.

"Excuse me, boys," he said, and greeted us. Then he took from his pocket a student certificate, opened it and read aloud: "Gulika, daughter of David Tchibadze, student in the faculty of economics, third year. Your certificate, lady!" and he laid it on the table.

"Thank you. Please sit down," Gulika said.

"Thank you, but they are waiting for me," he said, putting his hand on his heart.

"Teymo, you ask him!" Gulika turned to me.

"Please have a glass with us!" I said, and held out a glass to him.

"This is my Teymuri, and this is Guram Tchitchinadze, the critic. He writes poems, too. Have you read *Nikortsmenda*?"

"No."

"Well, he wrote it," Gulika said and laughed.

"It has been a pleasure. Good health to all of you!"

"What's your name?" Gulika asked.

"Afto."

"Afthanddil is a nice name. You should use it. My fiancé is called Teymuraz. Is that girl over there your wife?" Gulika went on.

"Well, no!" Afto stuttered.

"Then, the wife of your friend?"

"No."

"Is she anybody's wife?"

"Good-bye." Afto tried to hurry away.

"She's nobody's wife! Do you hear, Teymo? She doesn't belong to anybody!"

"Good-bye, and thank you!" Afto said and hurried away.

I looked at the nearby table. Lia sat with her head bent. She was red as a beetroot, and she was tearing nervously at a pack of cigarettes.

"Aren't you ashamed of yourself, Gulika? She heard everything!"

Gulika paid no attention to me. She turned to Guram:

"Victory to all fools, all sympathetic idiots! To my Teymuri, the most sympathetic of all the sympathetic fools! Never in the history of mankind has there been such a red-gold fool like him—"

"Gulika, you are drunk!" Guram said.

Lia got up and went out of the café. The boys followed her.

"You are a fool too, but Teymuri is a bigger fool, and that is why I love him more than I love you."

"Gulika! Stop!" I said, and stood up.

Gulika took four hundred rubles out of her hand-bag and threw them on the table.

"I got some money from my mother today. I have two hundred left," she said, and then she went out.

"Follow her, if you are my friend!" I begged Guram.

Guram followed her. The whole café was looking at me. I went past all the tables and went up to Dursun.

"How are you, Dursun?" I said.

"Sit down!" he said, taking a sip of coffee.

"All that coffee will kill you, Dursun!"

"Death from what you love is pleasant."

"Who says that?"

"Whoever said it spoke the truth!"

"Bring cognac and coffee!" I shouted at the waiter.

The waiter brought the cognac and coffee and set them on the table. We sat in silence. I filled Dursun's glass. He drank, and held his glass out to me again. I filled it a second time, and he drank again. I drank coffee, while Dursun drank cognac. Thus, in silence, he drank nearly a half a bottle. I finished my coffee and turned the cup over on the saucer.

"Tell me the future, Dursun!"

"Impossible!"

"Why?"

"I don't know how to foretell the future."

"If you don't know, then who does?"

"Nobody!"

"Then why do you predict things for other people?"

"I cheat them."

"Do you cheat yourself, too?"

"It's because I can't cheat myself that I'm sitting here!"

"Cheat me, too!"

"No!"

"Why, Dursun, why?"

"It's impossible to cheat you. You have the eyes of an innocent child!" Dursun said, and stood up. "I'm leaving!"

"Wait, Dursun, predict something for me—in spite of everything!" I took him by the sleeve and made him sit down.

"Well," he said, and took my cup. "Where do you live?"

"I'm from Tiflis."

"Tiflis is no address! I know perfectly well that you are not from here. Where are you staying in Batum?"

"At the hotel."

"What do you want from me, my son?" he said suddenly.

I was at a loss. "I don't want anything from you, Dursun!"

"Then leave me alone!" he said, and put the cup back down on the saucer.

"Don't you want to tell my fortune?"

"I told you before—I don't want to cheat you."

"Cheat me!"

Dursun bent his head. He was silent for a long time. Then he began dully, very dully, his hoarse, cracked voice sending an unpleasant shiver through my body.

"Now . . . that red-haired woman who is with you will become your wife. She isn't your wife yet?"

"No."

"Well, she will be!" Dursun turned the cup around

in his hands, and bent over it slightly. He looked at
the sediment on the bottom for a little while, and
then went on.

"You will have children . . . a girl and a boy. First
a girl and then a boy. You will have a good position,
you will have a pretty wife, pretty children, and there
will be no man in the world happier than you—for
one, two, three, ten years." Dursun put down the cup,
rested his head on both hands, closed his eyes and fell
silent.

"And what happens after that, Dursun?"

"After that you will lose your pretty wife. Your
pretty wife will follow a ship, a huge white ship.
You will begin to search for your wife, and you
will know that your friend spat on your soul. Then
you will begin to seek death, but death will not come
to you, because death doesn't need you. Your soul
will have already left your body. Then every trace
of you will vanish—your name, love, brother, friend,
son, seed and fruit. You will say it is not worthwhile to live, and you will put your head into a
noose, but someone will untie the noose. Then you
will decide it is not worthwhile to die, because there's
nothing in the world worth giving your life for."
Dursun grew silent again.

"And afterward, Dursun?" I asked. I felt my voice
trembling.

"Afterward you will not care about anything. First
you will not care about yourself, later you will not
care about the whole world. You will become another person completely."

"Who?"

"You will become me, Dursun. You will find a
place, and like me you will look in the bottom of
coffee cups for something that nobody can find—
something that cannot be found. You will be like me.
You will be nothing!" Dursun fell silent again and
I knew he had nothing more to say.

A man was facing me, or rather, not a man, but

something that God had once created from clay,
breathed a soul into, and then, for the sake of an
apple, He had sacrificed and surrendered it, without
leaving it any protection under the enormous sky.

"It is a lie!" I said.

"What is a lie?" Dursun asked, and looked at me
with a blank expression.

"Everything you have said is a lie!"

"I didn't say anything," Dursun shook his head.

"What do you mean? You said that nothing, neither
friend, nor love, nor anything else exists—is worth
dying for!"

"I didn't say anything. I only predicted your future
—that's all!" Dursun said obstinately. "I said nothing.
I told you nothing. Everything exists—love, friends,
life, death, happiness, joy—everything! That's all I
said to you!"

"I have a friend who will never spit on my soul."

"You are still very young," Dursun smiled.

"I am not very young!"

"You are a fledgling," Dursun said.

"You lie!"

"But I told you I would cheat you."

"No, you told me the truth."

"If I told you the truth, what more do you want
from me?"

"But you don't believe in anything, and so I cannot
agree with you!"

"Very well! Believe in whatever you want! The
world is full of icons."

"I want only one icon!"

"Then take it!"

"Please give me some advice."

"No!"

"You don't believe in anything? Neither icon nor
God?"

"No."

"You are a miserable creature! A beggar! A cow-
ard!"

"If there were a God, he would not have created me. There is no God!"

"There is a God."

"What do you call God?" Dursun said.

"Love, goodness, truth, mother, friend . . . and you deny all that, Dursun?"

Dursun's chin began to tremble, his eyes filled with tears. He stood up and I stood up, too. He took the coffee cup in a trembling hand and smashed it on the table. The cup crumbled to dust. He smashed a second, a third, a fourth. With both hands he grabbed me by the shoulders and shook me.

"And yet there is no God! No! No God, do you hear? Do you hear?" he shouted.

Then he loosened his grip and leaned weeping on the table. I put some money on the saucer and went out of the café.

It was raining outside. I crossed the boulevard and came to the sea. The rain fell in sheets, but it was warm, very warm. It grew darker. Suddenly the huge eye of the searchlight tore through the thick curtain of rain and illuminated the whole sea. It moved for a moment, toward the shore, then back to the sea, and finally went out altogether.

In a short while the searchlight appeared again, and again tore through the curtain of rain, and again lay over the shore. I walked on in the darkness and sat down in the sand. The sea was rustling, rustling. One could imagine that millions of people with nothing better to do had come to the beach and were throwing sand into the sea by handfuls. The sea was rustling, rustling. The rain was torrential.

"Teymo!" I suddenly heard the voice of Guram. "Teymo!" I did not answer. "Teymo!" the voice came closer.

I had taken off my shirt and was sitting there naked from the waist up.

A thousand, ten thousand, a hundred thousand fingers of rain beat on my body. "Teymo!" Guram's voice came closer and soon I heard his footsteps, first from afar and then close beside me. "There you are!"

"What do you want with me?"

"Are you mad?"

"Sit down!"

"Where?"

"Here beside me!"

"Get up! Don't be ridiculous! Why did you take off your shirt?" Guram said, and gripped my arm.

"Sit down. I have to talk to you."

"Do you think I'm a deep-sea diver? Let's go! We can talk in the hotel." He pulled at my arm.

"Would you spit on my soul? " I asked him.

"I knew you were a fool, but I did not know you were mad!"

"I am asking you! Would you spit on my soul?"

"Get up, or I'll go without you!"

"Go!"

"And what will I say to Gulika?"

"Say that I'm mad!"

"That she knows already!"

"Then say that you couldn't find me!"

"Get up. This is too much! I'm getting wet."

"Sit down. You can't get any wetter."

"What have you drunk to make you so stupid? God damn it! Didn't we drink the same thing?" Guram said, and he sat down by my side.

"Now, what do you want?"

"What is Gulika doing?"

"Crying."

"Let her cry. That's not such a bad thing. Dursun cries, too."

"Who?"

"Dursun."

"Dursun is a drunkard," Guram laughed.

"You are a drunkard!" I said.

"What do you want? If you insist on committing

suicide, it's not my fault. Let me go back to the hotel!" Guram implored.

"Have you ever seen a man who doesn't believe in anything in this world?"

"You!" Guram said. "You believe in neither God nor friend. You force me to sit out in this rain. You are killing me, and I am a completely innocent man!"

"Do you believe in anything?"

"What, for example?"

"Something!"

"And what do you suppose 'something' means?" Guram asked.

"Friendship, love, hate, happiness, misfortune. What do you believe in, and what don't you believe in?"

"Is this the time for that sort of thing, Teymo?" Guram said, looking up at the low clouds.

"Tell me!" I shouted. "What do you love in the whole world?"

"Wine, the sound of flutes, tobacco, women!" grinned Guram.

"I ask you. Please answer me!"

"My mother and father."

"What else?"

"Life, joy, happiness!"

"What else?"

"Oh, besides that I love the sun, the sea . . ."

"Anything more?"

"Sure! I love you, you Tartar! But get up and go in now," Guram said.

"Would you ever spit on my soul?"

"No, of course not!"

"Never?"

"Never!"

"Even if I spat on your soul? Even then you still wouldn't?" I asked Guram. He was silent.

"Why are you silent?"

"You must not spit on my soul," he said.

"But if I did?"

"No, no, no! Do you hear! You must not spit on me!" Guram jumped up.

"Suppose I did, what then? What would you do?"

Guram grew silent again. Finally he sat down and put his heavy arm on my shoulder. "Then I would spit in your face, too."

"On my soul?"

"In your face! In your face!"

"And after that?"

"After that, if you keep on asking me such questions, I will break your jaw and your spine!" Guram said, and I knew he would do at least half of what he had promised if I continued to try his patience.

The rain stopped. The searchlight swept over the sea more insistently. The sea boiled up like a huge cauldron, spilling a yellow foam on the coast.

I got up, and so did Guram. We went to the hotel. Nobody was in the lobby, but the short-haired Afto was standing at the telephone on the manager's desk and talking to someone. Involuntarily I stopped and listened.

"I am on my knees to you—" Afto was saying.

"Let's go," Guram said to me.

"You go on. I'll catch up with you."

Guram looked at me strangely, but went away.

"Let me see you for one minute!" Afto continued, looking at his watch. "I'll come to you . . . your morning never ends! . . . I can't stand any more either! . . . Wait. Maybe you don't want to, but I do! Why do you do this?" Afto suddenly hung up the receiver and started to dial again.

I went upstairs. When I reached the first-floor lobby I turned to the right. Ninety-eight, one hundred and two . . . Here are the even numbers, and the odd numbers are on the other side. A hundred and one, a hundred and three, a hundred and five . . . A hundred and five. My heart contracted. I must knock on the door of one hundred and five. I lifted my hand, but then did not dare to knock. I heard the beating of my own heart. I also heard the telephone ringing in the room . . . ringing, ringing uninterruptedly and insistently . . . and I knew that it was Afto trying to call. But Lia did not lift the receiver. The ringing stopped, then began again, and this time Lia answered.

"Listen!" she began.

Again my heart contracted. My mouth was dry. My hand trembled as I knocked at the door. There was sudden silence in the room. I knocked again.

"Who's there?" I heard from the room.

"Me!" I couldn't think of anything else to say.

"Who are you?"

"I'm Teymuri." The telephone rang again. "Lia, please open the door, I beg you."

"Go away!"

"Lia, just for one minute! I want to tell you something, and then I'll go!"

"Go away, or I'll call the manager!"

"Just one word!"

"What do you want?"

"Open the door!"

"Tell me from there!"

"I can't from here. Let me in!"

"Go away! Otherwise I'll call the manager right now!"

I heard her footsteps. Blood rushed to my face. "Lia!"

"Tell me what you want!"

"Your Afto is scum! A wretch! A monkey!"

"Which Afto?"

"That one, your Afto, the one who's ringing you now!"

"He is not my Afto!"

"Whoever he is, he's a wretch! He doesn't love you!"

"I know!"

"He says that you . . . that you . . ."

"That I what?"

"That you attached yourself to him!" I stopped, and waited for an answer. My heart seemed to come up to my throat and stick there, choking me. Lia did not speak. I went on: "Your Afto is a fool! He believes in nothing in the world, neither in you nor in any of his friends! He spat on your soul today, in front of me, before you arrived at the café. I don't want anything from you! I only want you to know that Afto is a wretch! You must not love such garbage!"

"Go away, Teymuri! You are drunk!"

"I know! But even so, your Afto is a wretch!"

"Go!" Lia said, but in such a low voice that I was surprised I could hear it.

I said what I had to say, and now there was nothing for me to do but to leave. I rubbed my ice-cold hand over my wet forehead and face. When I opened my eyes and turned around, I saw, standing in front of me, Afto, pale with anger. But he was smiling.

"How are you? I got terribly wet," I said clumsily. To hide my confusion I began to roll down the wet and crumpled sleeves of my shirt. At the same time, my whole body was tense with waiting for what would happen next.

Afto stood straight as an arrow. Suddenly he moved. I jerked my head aside and his fist went past my ear. In a fury he flung himself at me. I stumbled, caught my toe on the carpet and fell on my back. I jumped up fast as lightning, but before I could pull myself together, I felt a terrible pain between the eyes and I fell again. Once more I jumped to my feet, but I could not see anything. With both hands Afto grabbed me by the shirt and shoved me back against the wall. Little by little I regained consciousness. Now Afto slapped me in the face. The blood pounded in my temples until I thought the veins would burst. Before Afto could slap me again I gripped his shoulders, pulled him toward me, and, with all the force I had left, I hit him with my head. Afto groaned, leaned against my chest and then

fell on both knees before me, still clutching my shirt.
I couldn't loosen his grip, so I simply pulled away,
leaving half my shirt in his hands.

"Get up!" I said to the fallen Afto.

He did not answer, but covered his face with his
hands and lay in the same position.

"Get up!" I repeated, and seized him by the shoulders.

He got up first on one knee and then on the other.
I backed away. He straightened up and looked at me
for a long time with a blank expression.

"I will meet you somewhere!" he said in a flat
voice, and wiped the blood from his cut lip.

"Wherever you wish!" I replied.

He turned around and went along the hall. Then
he stopped, turned again to me and said: "I wouldn't
be a man if I didn't pay you back for this!"

"Go away! You don't frighten me!"

"We will see!" he smiled, looking askance at me.

"We will see!" I said. He turned and went.

I went up to the third floor. Before entering my
room, I knocked at Gulika's door.

"Who's there?" I heard from inside.

"Gulika, it's Teymuri! Open the door!"

"I'm in bed!"

"Never mind! Open the door!"

"Come back tomorrow morning. I'm sleeping now."

"Not tomorrow morning! Now!"

The door opened. Gulika was not in bed. When she
saw me bruised, with my shirt torn, she stepped back
in surprise.

"What happened to you?"

"Sit down," I said.

Gulika sat down on the bed without taking her
eyes from me.

"What happened?"

"I just had a fight with that idiot," I said, and
lit a cigarette. I inhaled.

When I looked again at the cigarette I noticed that I had cut my lip, the cigarette was covered with blood.

"What idiot?" she asked, astonished.

"That short-haired idiot!"

"Why?"

"I don't know."

"Over that flashy girl?"

"Yes."

"And then you have the nerve to come here and tell me all about it?"

"He is saying she is a bitch!"

"What does that matter to you?"

"Well, who else does it matter to?"

"Do you think that is any of your business?"

"I know she is a decent girl!"

"And just how do you know this?" Gulika laughed ironically.

"I don't really know! But I can tell!"

"You don't know, you only suppose."

"Some people probably consider you a bitch too, because you're here with me."

"In the first place, I am not here with you! And second, I don't care in the least about that!"

"You don't care what people think about you?"

"No!" Gulika said.

"Well, I care!"

"You came to the conclusion that this woman is decent, and you come to me to tell me all about it?" Gulika said and she laughed sarcastically.

"No, I went to her, and told her that the short-haired boy is a wretch and a monkey."

"And then?"

"Then I met him, and we fought."

"What do you want from me now?" Gulika asked. She stood up.

"I want you to get up and come with me to Tiflis."

"Why?"

"I don't want to stay here any longer!"

"Are you afraid?"

"Yes, I'm afraid," I said.

"Are you afraid of that boy?"

"No, I'm afraid of myself!"

"I'm not going anywhere! Go away! I have to sleep."

"Get up and come with me! The train leaves at twelve."

"I will not!" Gulika said obstinately, and she sat down.

"If you loved me, you would stand up immediately and come with me."

"No."

"All right! I'm guilty! Forgive me for what happened, only get up and come with me to Tiflis."

"I'm not afraid of anybody, neither am I afraid of falling in love with anybody! Therefore, I will not go!" Gulika said.

"Do you think I am leaving because I'm afraid of falling in love with Lia?" I asked.

"Yes!" Gulika said, looking straight into my eyes. She was right. I had no answer. I lit the cigarette again and remained silent. We sat like this for a long time. Finally I stood up. Gulika did not move.

"Then I will go alone!" I said.

"Go!" Gulika said, without looking at me.

I went to my room. Guram was asleep. I walked in on tiptoe and carefully dragged my suitcase from under the bed. I changed my clothes and walked out on tiptoe. I looked at the clock in the hall—it was ten minutes after eleven. Loud singing could be heard coming from the restaurant. I went down to the lobby. The manager was sitting in his booth, dozing.

"Sasha!" I said in a low voice.

"There is no room!" the manager rubbed his face. When he saw me his eyes opened wide.

"Give me my passport!"

"Look at yourself. What is the matter with you?" he asked in astonishment.

"I'll be late for the train! Please give me my passport!"

"Are you leaving?"

"Only me!"

"Did you have a fight?"

"No!"

"Then what's the matter with you?"

"Are you a doctor or are you a hotel manager? Give me the passport!"

"I'm in my own field. I'm a doctor and an engineer and everything else!"

"Are you going to give me my passport?"

The manager looked in his desk for my passport and handed it to me.

"Are you going to pay the bill, or is your friend going to do it?"

"My friend!"

"Still, what happened to you?"

"I bumped into a tree!"

"Couldn't you avoid it?"

"I could not!"

"Does this happen to you often?"

"Often!"

"You would have a nice time if you entered a forest!"

"Good night!"

"Keep well, and please stay on the sidewalk! There are so many trees that you would breathe your last before reaching the railroad station!" the manager said.

"I will try, sir," I said.

"Be brave!" Sasha held out his hand. Suddenly he said: "Do you want me to read you the poem I wrote yesterday?"

"Is it long?" I asked, looking at my watch. I had twenty minutes until the train left.

"No."

"Please don't make me late!" I begged him.

"Well, here it is!

The Black Sea is good during a storm,
It seems to be drunk, though it drinks no wine.
Every minute, every day, and in the evening time,
Long live the foaming angry, love-agitated sea!

Now, when it is night, and raining outside,
I watch day and night the Intourist Hotel.
Outside the wind, the wind, the wind blows.
We are four: I, the Black Sea, Batum, and the Wind.

"What do you say?" Sasha said in a careful voice.
"Somehow it reminds me of Galaktioni, you sly
one," I said, wagging my finger at him.
"Is that bad?" he said, pleased by the comparison.
"On the contrary, it's good!" I said, and slapped
him on the shoulder.
"Well, be a good boy," he said, "and when you get
to Tiflis, take it to the editor of *Mnathobi*. Tell him
I sent it. Don't be shy, he knows me. He stays with
me at the Intourist Hotel almost every year."
"Yes, I'll do that!"
"Tell him to send the honorarium here at the In-
tourist Hotel. Oh yes, and tell him to print the poem
under a pseudonym!"
"What pseudonym?"
"He knows."
"Does he?"
"It's the Dolphin."
"Wouldn't North Star be better?" I said.
"My dear fellow, do what you are told!" Sasha
said, looking at me suspiciously.
"Whatever you say! Good night!" I held out my
hand to Sasha.
"Good night!" he said and shook my hand.
I put his poem into my pocket and left the hotel.

Abibo

———

Abibo Thodria lives on the ground floor of our home. They say that he was a friend of my father and that when I was little he used to put me on his shoulders, pretend to be my horse and gallop around the room. I, of course, do not remember this. However, I well remember meeting Abibo in the hall, just after armbands for uniforms were introduced. He was dressed in high leather boots and a tunic adorned with armbands. On each armband he had two stars. I guessed that he was a lieutenant colonel, because I remember seeing examples of the new insignia in the newspapers. I ran down the stairs holding my bread ration card.

"Where are you going?" he asked me with a smile.

"For bread."

"Are you hungry?"

"Not yet."

"Are you usually hungry?"

I did not understand what he wanted to know, so I just shrugged.

"What do you hear about your mother?"

"Nothing."

"And your father?"

"Nothing."

"Why is your skin so yellow? Are you ill?"

"No."

"Have you been ill?"

"Yes."

"With what?"

"Pleurisy!"

"Did you take a sulfa drug?"

"No."

"Why?"

"I couldn't afford it. It's very expensive."

"Yes, it is expensive. Are you studying?"

"Yes."

"How is it going?"

"Very well."

"In any case, you must try to be useful. Your parents compromised themselves, and . . ." Abibo was gone.

Abibo always met me on the stairs, either in the morning or the evening, and he always asked me, "How are you, boy?"

"Fine, Uncle Abibo!"

"Are you hungry? If you're hungry, don't be ashamed to tell me. Have you eaten anything today?"

"No."

"Why not? You must eat! Do you have a fever? Your eyes are blinking strangely."

"No."

"Are you studying?"

"Yes."

"Have you been accepted in the Young Communist League?"

"Yes."

"Well, be brave!"

And so it always was.

I met Abibo on the stairs as usual one week after my mother returned. He was just opening his door. His face lit up as soon as he saw me.

"Greetings, Teymuraz!"

"How are you, Uncle Abibo?"

"Come in, boy! Aren't you ashamed to grow to be such a big man and never show your face in my humble lodging? Come in now!" and before I could say anything, he slapped me on the shoulder and drew me into the room.

"Sit down!" he said, and made me sit at the table, which was covered with a heavy cloth.

I sat and looked around. Abibo had gone into the other room. The room where I sat had a huge sideboard like one I saw in the restaurant of the Shorapani railroad station. There were silver and gold-plated vessels on the sideboard, and also—at the ends and in the middle—there were two large crystal flower-bowls, one bowl made in the form of a ship. They were filled with fruit, but were so far from me that they seemed to be still lifes. To my right a carpet hung on the wall. It was so huge that it covered the wall and part of the floor. A large pair of antlers, hung with various weapons—daggers and so on—hung over the carpet, and slightly below this there was a framed picture of a lovely woman and a moustached man wearing a tall Caucasian hat. This picture was placed between two crossed, silver-plated swords.

There was a desk in front of me, with a white marble desk set, apparently never used. A marble bust of a fat man stood beside the set. Behind the desk was a bookcase full of books. In addition, the room held a black grand piano with white elephants on it.

I could not make head or tail of what was going on in the other room. Suddenly the door opened, and Abibo came in. He was wearing blue and white striped pajamas, a tall winter hat on his head, and slippers on his feet. He looked very much like an escaped convict. In each hand he held a thimble-sized coffee cup, which he put down on the round table. He took a bottle of cognac from a desk drawer and a bowl of fruit from the sideboard, put them on the table and finally sat down beside me.

"What do you say?" Abibo asked me.

"What is there to say?"

"Do you feel stronger now?"

"Not so bad!"

"Well, let's each have a drink!" he said, and poured the cognac.

We drank. I started looking around the room again.

"My father," he said, indicating the man in the picture.

"You look very much like him."

"He's my father."

"How could it be otherwise?"

"I heard that your mother has arrived," Abibo said suddenly, catching my eye.

"Yes, a week ago," I answered, and looked away.

"And what about the poor woman?" Abibo peered at me.

"Nothing."

"Does she tell you anything?"

"Nothing!" I shook my head.

"Absolutely nothing?"

"Sometimes a little bit."

"What, for instance?"

"That they were in great need there."

"And then?"

"Then nothing more."

"But still . . . ?"

"She said, 'I didn't know why I was punished.'"

"She didn't know?"

"No."

"Did she meet your father?"

"Where?"

"There."

"No."

"Has she said anything about me?" Abibo asked.

"What could she say about you?"

"Well, hasn't she asked about me?"

"Yes."

"What did she say?" Abibo asked, and he bent his whole body toward me.

"'How did he escape, poor man?'"

"Yes, yes," Abibo shook his head, and again poured some cognac into the glasses. "What else does she say?"

"Nothing else! What could she say? She just sits and reads all day."

"What does she read?"

"Everything she can find!"

"Then . . . she didn't say anything else about me?" Abibo said, watching me carefully.

"Nothing else! Why? Do you know anything, Uncle Abibo?" I asked him.

"What should I know, boy?" Abibo frowned.

"I didn't know! You badger me with questions— What did she say about me? What did she . . . ?"

"What do you mean by badger, boy? I ask only out of curiosity. Can't a neighbor be interested in a neighbor's life?"

"Yes . . . well then, please come and see her. If she has anything to say, she will tell you herself!"

"I'll come when I possibly can."

"I must go now, Uncle Abibo."

"Go then."

I stood up and went to the door. "Good-bye," I said.

"Good-bye!" Abibo said. "Wait!" He stopped me. "Don't say anything to your mother! Don't even say you were with me. She'll remember the old times, the old days, and that will make her sad. Do you understand?" These last words were not merely said, but took the form of commands. His eyes pierced me. A shudder ran through my body.

"Now go!" he said, and drank some cognac straight from the bottle.

I closed the door.

Thavera

___

"Get up, son! Some man is asking to see you," Mother awakened me.

Surprised, I got up and put on my trousers.

"Whoever it is, tell him to come in," I said.

"He doesn't want to come in. He says he wants to see you for only a minute," Mother said, and looked at me with frightened eyes.

I went out into the hall, which was darker than my room. A medium-sized man with a cap pulled over his eyes stood at the door. He held a small suitcase in his hand.

"You want to see me?" I said.

"Teymo, excuse me! I thought you were alone.

Now I've seen you and I will go," the unknown man replied.

His voice seemed very familiar to me, but in spite of that I could not recognize him.

"Don't you recognize me?"

"I'm sorry, but I don't recognize you."

The unknown laughed. By God, where had I seen this smile? It's very much like . . . the ninth class! No . . . the last bench at the back of the classroom? The long recess? The game of knucklebones, the pipe, the organ, Thavera's doves, Ramaz Korsaveli, Thavera, Thavera, Thavera!

"Thavera!" I shouted, and embraced my long-lost school friend. "Thavera, is it you, old fellow? Come in, Thavera. Where have you been? Where, Thavera? Is it possible that you're really here?"

Thavera nodded his head, and smiled awkwardly. I dragged him into the room and made him sit down on my bed.

"Mother, do you have anything for him to eat? This is my mother," I said to Thavera. He stood up and bowed.

"Sit down, my child!" Mother said to him. She went to the kitchen.

"Where have you come from, Thavera? Tell me how you are! Did they release you just now?" I asked him, and began to unbutton his coat.

"How are you, Teymo?"

"Not too bad!"

"Well, I've seen you, and I will go now."

"Are you crazy? Where do you have to go? Mother, are you bringing something?"

"Teymo, I will come back and see you tomorrow. I have something very important to talk to you about."

"What is it? Tell me now!"

My mother came into the room. She put bread, cheese and onions on the table, and then sat down.

"Eat, Thavera! You're probably hungry."

"Thank you," Thavera said, without having to be

asked twice. He ate quietly and with self-restraint. I guessed that he was very hungry, but did not want to show his weakness. I did not ask any questions, nor did he say anything. When he finished eating, he took out a pack of cigarettes and offered me one. We lit our cigarettes, and exhaled.

"Now tell me what you have to say," I said.

"I must go," Thavera insisted.

Mother looked at us in amazement.

"He is my schoolmate, Mother. Do you remember Ramaz Korsaveli? Thavera is his nickname."

Mother smiled, but she did not remember.

"How can you possibly not remember Thavera Korsaveli, who had the doves? He gave me two homing pigeons as a gift. We studied together from the first grade!"

"I don't remember, son," my mother said quietly. She stood up and went to the balcony.

"I will lie down here and you may sit on my bed."

"I will go, ma'am!" Thavera said.

"Please stay, son," Mother smiled at him.

Mother lay down. Thavera and I sat facing each other. I did not take my eyes off him. He gathered up the bread crumbs with the point of his knife, divided them into two mounds, then pushed them together again, and so on.

"Speak, Thavera!" I said, and settled myself to listen.

"I'm fed up with my situation, Teymo. I can't stand any more. Ten years is too much."

A terrible premonition ran through my mind.

"I've had enough, this six years. Four years more will mean the end of me. I need neither their rights, nor their tolerance, nor their praise for good behavior. I am no thief! I've had enough! Either they believe me now, or I die. It's impossible to endure any more. I've had it!"

"Thavera, did you run away?" I waited fearfully for his answer.

"I, and Guijo, Guivi, Lamaz Vaho, and Iracha."

"How?"

"A car was standing in the yard. The key was inside. It stood there for half an hour . . . Then Guijo got behind the wheel. I sat beside him, Guivi, Lamaz Vaho and Iracha lay down in the back. Guijo started the engine—nobody paid any attention. He backed up, then put the car in first, second, and finally in third. We hit the gate head-on. It broke open and we were gone. They opened fire from all the turrets, but they were too surprised to move after us. Before they could collect themselves we were already on the Kakhethi road. We abandoned the car there. Lamaz Vaho and Iracha were killed. Lamaz Vaho got his skull blown off."

Thavera stood up. "We went in different directions. That was three days ago," he said. He bent the knife until it broke in his hand. "Now they're looking for me. I can't take any more. I cannot endure another four years there. They must believe me, or it will be the end of my life!" Thavera got up, then sat down again. He was silent. I wiped the cold sweat from my forehead, then I got up and started walking around the room.

"They're searching for me now. I am here with you, I have seen you, and I can go now. I want you to know that I didn't run away just because it was bad there. I also want to study, to sleep in a warm bed, to work decently. It's enough for me. In four years life may end. Either they will believe me or I will kill myself, but I won't go back there!"

"Sit down!" I said to him. Thavera sat.

"We must think of something!" I said, and then I laughed at my own words. What could I think of?

"What can we do?" Thavera said. As if he guessed my secret thoughts, he smiled bitterly.

Thavera was again playing with the bread crumbs. I put the two parts of the broken knife together. The knife seemed to be perfectly sound, there was no sign of the break. But when I took one hand away the blade fell on the table with a clatter, and only the handle was left. We sat that way for a long time. I could not think of anything else to do. I looked at Thavera. He sat there with his head bent.

"Mother!" I called in a low voice.

"Yes, my dear?" Mother answered from the balcony.

"Did you hear?"

"I did."

"Did you hear everything?"

"Everything."

I looked at Thavera. He didn't raise his head.

"What do we do now, Mother?"

My mother fell silent. She thought for a long time. When she did not answer, Thavera lifted his head and looked hopefully in her direction. His eyes were full of expectation. He took a cigarette. I noticed how his hands trembled as he lighted it.

"Well, Mother?" I couldn't endure waiting any longer.

"It's a very difficult thing, my son," Mother said finally. "I don't know, but I think that such cases are never pardoned."

"Why?" I asked, and looked up at Thavera.

"I don't know why, but such things are not forgiven."

"But if he wants to study, if he swears never to steal again, if he cannot endure such a life?"

"Every prisoner says this, but nobody believes it," Mother said sadly.

"Why?"

"I don't know. Probably because not everyone is to be trusted."

"Thavera is not everyone! I know Thavera is telling the truth!"

"It doesn't matter that you know. No one is going to ask for your opinion," my mother said.

I was growing angry.

"So what, if nobody asks for my opinion. You are afraid of everything, you don't believe in anything! To every question, your answer is always no, or I don't know! I will go to everyone, I will plead, explain, beg, show that Thavera could be a very useful man! I will even go to Abibo . . . !"

"Go then, my son," my mother said in a low voice. She took no further part in the conversation.

"Don't be afraid, Thavera! We will do something. We will think it over some more, then tomorrow morning I will go to Abibo."

"Who is Abibo?"

"Abibo is a lieutenant colonel."

"Your mother is right. There's nothing to be done. I wrote at least a hundred petitions," he said, and explained everything in detail. "Either they didn't read them, or they didn't believe them."

"My mother can't possibly know what is necessary for you. I will go ask Abibo. If you like, I will go immediately. After all, he is a man! He will understand and say either yes or no. Do you want me to take you to him?"

"No! It is absolutely impossible for me to go to him!"

"Then you must stay here in my room. Don't go anywhere!"

"For me to go out is to be killed!" Thavera smiled bitterly.

"I'll go and tell him everything. Mother, I'm going!"

"Don't tell him where Thavera is!" my mother warned me.

I went downstairs, but when I got to Abibo's door I hesitated. Perhaps it would be better to see him tomorrow? Perhaps it would be better to say nothing to this man? Perhaps. But I don't know anyone else. What can I do? What other choice is there for Thavera? He himself said: "I will be killed in the street, or if they don't believe me, I will commit suicide!"

No, there is no other way—neither for Thavera, nor for me. I pressed the doorbell.

After a short time I heard the sound of slippers and the hoarse voice of Abibo.

"Who is there?"

"Me, Uncle Abibo! Teymuri!"

"What are you up to?"

"I have something to discuss with you! Something urgent!"

The door, closed with a chain, opened slightly. Abibo stuck out his nose. He seemed rather surprised. He examined me carefully and then he said: "Are you alone?"

"Quite alone!"

Abibo removed the chain and opened the door.

"Come in," he said.

I entered the room. "I'm sorry to bother you, Uncle Abibo, but it's something important!" Abibo sat down at his desk, turned off the biggest light and switched on the desk lamp. I was plunged into darkness.

"Turn on another light. I can't see anything!" I said.

Abibo turned on another lamp. I came closer to the desk and sat down before him.

"What's the matter?"

I hesitated again, to tell him or not? Maybe it's not worthwhile. Don't tell! Don't tell! Don't tell!— these two words beat in my head like a hammer. Tell! Tell! Tell!—my heart throbbed.

"Can't you speak?" Abibo asked me, and moved his chair noisily.

I decided to tell him. I swallowed nervously.

"Uncle Abibo, three days ago some prisoners escaped from the camp in a stolen car."

"I know this," Abibo said. His eyes flashed.

Oh God! What blue and burning eyes this man has! So clear that I can almost see through his head! How is it possible not to trust a man who has eyes like this? I was thinking.

"There were five of them: Guivi, Guijo, Lamaz Vaho, Iracha and Thavera—Ramaz Korsaveli."

"I know that! What else?" Abibo said impatiently.

"Two of the five were killed—Iracha and Lamaz Vaho."

"I know that, too."

"Of the other three, one is my schoolmate."

"The last name?"

"Korsaveli."

"First name?"

"Ramaz-Thavera."

"Where is he?" Abibo said so unexpectedly that I was tongue-tied.

"Where is he? I don't know where he is now. I saw him early this morning. Then . . . Where he is now I don't know."

"Don't you know?" he said, and I felt I was being investigated.

"I don't know where he is now!" I said with great difficulty, clearing my throat.

"What do you want, then?"

"Uncle Abibo, Thavera and I were students together. Thavera has already been in prison for six years! He can't stand it any longer! Thavera told me that during these six years he wrote a hundred petitions. Either nobody read them, or nobody believed them. He says that he can't take any more, that he will never steal again, that he wants to study, to live peacefully. He has no one to help him. He doesn't know what to do, where to go. 'Either I must be believed, or I will kill myself!' he told me. He swears he cannot endure the four remaining years of his sentence. Now he has no one to help him except me. And I have nobody except you!"

"He doesn't have any other protector besides you?" Abibo asked.

"No."

"And he came to you for help?"

"Yes."

"And you came to me at midnight?" Abibo said.

I could not meet Abibo's eyes. I bent my head.

"And now you don't know where he is?" Abibo persisted.

"I told him about you! What a good man you are! I said you would help him and believe in him."

"Why didn't he come himself?"

"He didn't dare!"

"He asks to be pardoned?"

"He asks to be heard and to be believed—he doesn't want to steal anymore. He wants to live decently and in peace."

"Does he really want that?"

"Uncle Abibo, do you believe me?" I said suddenly. Abibo apparently did not expect such a question. He hesitated. "Do you believe me, Uncle Abibo?" I repeated.

"About what?"

"In general."

"In general, you are a good boy, and why shouldn't I believe you?"

"Well, Thavera is better than I am! When we were students he was always the first in the class. He has nine school awards for good conduct and progress. He made only one mistake. Shouldn't he be forgiven? Shouldn't he be believed? If you believe in me you must believe in Thavera, too! Uncle Abibo, do what you would do if I were in his place! Everyone would believe you! Everyone respects you!"

"Tomorrow!" Abibo said, and turned out the light.

"What about tomorrow?" I asked.

"Tomorrow I will know everything! Tomorrow evening!"

I could not see Abibo's face. The room was in darkness.

"Should I come here tomorrow, Uncle Abibo?" I asked, and rose to go.

"Tomorrow evening!" Abibo lighted the main lamp

in the room. He stood with his back to me. When he
turned, he had the same quiet face, the same blue
transparent eyes.

"Tomorrow!" he said, and opened the door.

It is the last lecture of the day: the history of
Georgia. It is half past eight. In fifteen minutes the
lecture will be finished. Thavera is sitting at home
now, waiting for me. Abibo will be off duty by now,
and he too is waiting for me. My mother is sitting at
the window in the kitchen; she is watching the clock
and the street. She, more than anyone else, is waiting
for me. A short professor is standing on the rostrum.
He lectures very well; there is never an empty place
in the lecture hall when he is speaking. The audi-
torium is like a beehive.

". . . Vakhtang Gorgasali was a Goliath of a man.
The chronicler states that his height was twelve
hands . . ."

Guram and I are sitting together. Guram never
takes his eyes off the lecturer, but like me he is thinking about other things—probably about Thavera.
This morning I told him everything. He scolded me.
"You are an idiot!" he said. Gulika is sitting in front
of me, in the fourth row. Her red head sparkles like
a sun among so many black heads. From time to time
she takes notes on the lecture.

"The young king summoned the nobles and revealed to them his intention of invading the countries of the Alans, the Osetians and Khazars, in order
to release his sister, Gurandukht, who had been kid-
napped."

Gulika and I had not met since our return from
Batum. She was choked with feminine pride, and I
with masculine arrogance. She waited for me to break
down, and I waited for her. Guram had tried, several
times, to bring us together. Finally he said: "I, too,
have some pride!" and after that he left us alone.

Thavera is sitting and waiting for me. My mother waits, and Abibo waits too. Abibo knows everything by now.

". . . The Darial gorge was very narrow, and the army could not extend its forces. Therefore the opposing armies agreed to be represented by a champion from each side. The Khazars put forward a stupid giant called Tharkhan Khazar, and the Georgians put forward Pharsmun Pharukh. Tharkhan Khazar brandished his sword, and cleaved Pharsmun Pharukh in two, along with his horse. The Georgians were in despair until Vakhtang Gorgasali mounted his horse, and . . ."

"Didn't you say he was at your house?" Guram was asking me for what seemed to be the third time. I shook my head.

How good it would be if Thavera were sitting with us now! The university would not be changed, it would be the same university. Old Mosse would still stand at the doors and check Thavera's identification card, along with the rest, lest he should steal by without a card, and steal the others' share of knowledge. The manager of the dramatic club would be the same Vakhtang Mchedlishvili, and it is possible that he would allow Thavera to join. The dramatic club has been preparing a production of *Othello* for three years now; it is in great need of a curly-haired, deep-voiced student for the part of the Moor.

". . . As soon as the Alan and Khazar armies saw the giant Tharkhan Khazar's head cut off, they wavered and were terrified. But then the Osetians put forward the giant Baghatar, whose weight was too much for the strongest horse. 'Come to this side and fight me!' Baghatar shouted to Vakhtang. 'I am a king and you are a slave! You must come to me!' the young king shouted back. 'Very well. I shall come, but do not attack me while I am crossing the river!' Baghatar demanded an oath from the king . . ."

Thavera began to smoke when he was in the eighth

grade. We were in the eighth grade when Thavera
performed the role of Hitler in Roman Charekhishvili's play. The title of the play was *The Fall of Berlin*.

The Fall of Berlin
A historical drama in one act, two scenes.

Characters in the play:
Hitler—Ramaz Korsaveli
Goebbels—Vaja Tchanishvili
Goering—Archil Ergemlidze
Paulus—Pavle Ratiani
Eva Braun—Inola Tquemaladze
    Red Army men:
Lieutenant—Teymuraz Baramidze
1st Soldier—Guram Tchitchinadze
2nd—Nestor Djaparidze
3rd—Nodar Mikiashvili
Author—Roman Charekhishvili
Stage Manager—Instructor of the Pioneers, Lili
    Ugulava
Rehearsals every day from 6:00 P.M. to 9:00 P.M.
    in room 15 of the school clubhouse.
Première February 3. Admission gratis, by invita-
    tion.

The instructor of the Pioneers, Lili Ugulava—our
stage manager—had cast the roles and was sitting at
the head of the table.

"Roman, begin!" she says to the author.

The author opens the play in its thick binding,
coughs behind his hand and timidly begins.

"The action takes place in the Reichstag in Berlin.
At a long table are seated Goebbels, Goering, Paulus,
Eva Braun and Hitler. Only Hitler is standing. He
bites his nails and scratches his neck. He has eczema.
He is screaming like a madman. Occasionally the
crash of bombs is heard.

HITLER: I will raze all of Russia to the ground! I

will bring Stalin to his knees! Stalingrad will be mine within a week!

EVA: It will be yours, darling, of course it will be yours, only don't be so nervous! (*Eva tenderly strokes Adolf's cheek and gazes into his eyes with admiration. Hitler kisses her cheek and sits down.*)

GOEBBELS: My Führer! (*He rises.*) The position of our armies at Stalingrad is rather dubious. The mobilization of all our forces is necessary. Otherwise defeat is inevitable. I am afraid that—

HITLER: (*He jumps up foaming at the mouth and hits the table with his fist.*) Cowards! Are you afraid? Get out! Get out of the Reichstag! Cowards! Chicken-hearted sheep! You are sheep! Sheep!

GOERING: (*jumping up*) I am no sheep! I am not afraid!

HITLER: Come to me! I must kiss you! (*Goering goes up to him. Hitler hugs him. While Hitler is pressing Goering to his heart, Eva says to Goebbels:*)

EVA: Aren't you ashamed, Goebbels? Do you need to shatter his nerves any more? Don't you see he is completely mad?

GOEBBELS: Excuse me, lady. If it is impossible to tell the truth, then I prefer to be silent. (*Goebbels falls silent. Hitler stops kissing Goering and exclaims with enthusiasm:*)

HITLER: You will go to Stalingrad, my fat and faithful Goering!

GOERING: (*frightened*) I?

HITLER: You, not I! (*Goering turns pale.*)

GOERING: Beloved Hitler! My Führer needs me here! I would rather die than leave you. Paulus shall go to Stalingrad. (*Paulus' face is distorted with fear.*)

HITLER: Will you go?

PAULUS: I will. How can I not go? (*He whimpers.*)

HITLER: Most beloved. My dear one. Now my heart is relieved! (*He kisses first Eva, then Paulus. He takes off his medals and pins them on Paulus. Paulus cries.*)

PAULUS: My Führer, this is the happiest moment of

my life. I will go to Stalingrad; I will destroy the Communists, I will burn everything there, and I will try to capture Stalin. (*Eva applauds enthusiastically and jumps up.*)

EVA: (to Hitler) May I kiss Paulus?

HITLER: Kiss him! Kiss him! (*Eva kisses Paulus. Paulus, with frightened eyes, watches Hitler to see if he is jealous.*)

HITLER: Go to her! (*Encourages Paulus. Paulus kisses Eva. Hitler looks away.*)

PAULUS: (*after kissing*) I will show the Communists the importance and power of German arms. (*The crash of a bomb is heard. Paulus hides under the table. When the noise stops he comes out.*) I will plow Stalingrad under like Carthage, and if I don't return alive, be sure that my last word will be "My Führer"! (*He sits down and cries.*)

GOEBBELS: My Führer! Excuse me for having been so hopeless a few minutes ago. Now I am again optimistic and I publicly declare my faith in you! The days of Communism are numbered! Today or tomorrow Stalin will surrender and Russia will be our colony! Long live Germany!

HITLER: Come here! I must kiss you, too. (*Goebbels goes to him and they kiss each other. Eva pours wine into some tall glasses.*)

EVA: Gentlemen, long live Germany! Long live the Führer! (*They all drink and sing "Long live, long live" in German.*)

HITLER: Now go away! Eva and I want to sleep. (*Eva yawns, everyone goes, the light is turned off.*)

CURTAIN

The second scene is based mainly on sound effects and lighting. The action still takes place in Berlin, this time in the shelter. The devastation of Hitler's office is seen: his room is blown up, papers scattered everywhere. Flashes of light appear from time

to time. Four powerful ventilators produce a terrible
heat on the stage; backstage, a loud drum beats con-
tinuously. Suddenly, in the doorway of the office, I
appear with my soldiers, automatic rifles ready.

"Hands up, Hitler, Goering, Goebbels, Ribbentrop
and Eva!" I shout.

No sound comes from the office. Then I enter the
office with my gun in my hand, and what do I see?
On the floor lie Hitler, Eva and a big German
shepherd dog. Nearby there lies a vial of poison.

"They have poisoned themselves, the cowards!" I
say, and I laugh proudly.

"Comrades!" I begin my monologue. "The enemy
is destroyed in his own den. Good has defeated evil.
Private Tchitchinadze, deliver a message to Comrade
Zhukov! Tell him the war is over."

Guram gives me a military salute and goes out.
The performance comes to an end.

The dress rehearsal was attended by the Artistic
Council of Teachers and the Council of Parents.

"Close the door and let no one leave," the director
ordered. The doors were closed. First, the father of
Inola Tquemaladze took the floor.

"Honorable director," he began, "I do not think
we have brought up our child badly. She takes music
lessons and English lessons, shows great respect to
her elders and has the highest grades in school. How
do you explain the fact that she has been given the
part of Eva Braun, a corrupt woman who was the
concubine of mankind's most horrible enemy—that
scoundrel Hitler?"

"We are dealing with art, sir," the instructor of
the Pioneers replied.

"No, you are dealing in depravity! She was kissed
three times on the stage! Twice by Hitler and once
by Goebbels! I am removing her from this group
and from the school! Go, my child." And Eva was
taken away.

Archil Ergemlidze's father expressed his embarrassment that an old Bolshevik's son—and he was an old Bolshevik—should take the part of Goering, a role consisting chiefly of abuse and cursing Stalin and Communism. He suggested that it would be better if I, Teymuraz Baramidze, the son of a Trotskyist, played the part of Goering, while his son, Archil Ergemlidze, played the part of the Soviet officer.

The director noted the proposal.

The mother of Vaja Tchanishvili brought up the question of Goebbels' limp: "I don't want people to think my son is lame."

"But Goebbels was lame, madam!" the director explained to her.

"That doesn't matter. Half of Tiflis doesn't know that Goebbels was lame!"

One member of the Artistic Council expressed his doubts about the development of the plot.

"There are many kinds of episodes," he said, "which have been omitted from the difficult days of the Great Patriotic War. It is important to remark that Hitler looks very young, and for that reason he is not convincing. Besides, it is rather surprising that Hitler and the others should be speaking in Georgian. I think the entire first act should be omitted," he concluded.

"I don't like Hitler either!" the director replied. "You—Charekhishvili!" he said, turning suddenly to the colorless author. "Where did you get the words Hitler pronounces just before his death?"

"Those words, honorable professor, I invented myself."

"What right have you got to invent words which no one even heard? How do you know what Hitler was doing in his office?"

Charekhishvili could not remember who told him what Hitler was doing in his office, and he hung his head.

"Mr. Director! What is the point of being so pedantic about this whole matter? The children amuse themselves, they perform something on the stage, they write something—God bless them!" Nodar Mikiashvili's mother said.

"Of course you have nothing to worry about, madam! Your son plays the part of a Red Army man, whereas mine curses and scolds our government throughout the whole performance," the father of Paulus said, jumping to his feet.

"Aren't you ashamed of yourselves, comrades, to talk so much about this? How is it possible to take seriously a matter that concerns, after all, only a play put on by the eighth grade?" smiled one of the teachers.

Nevertheless, the play did not open as scheduled. The instructor of the Pioneers was severely admonished, and Roman Charekhishvili was forbidden to write any more plays about the Great Patriotic War.

"I wish that damned bell would ring! It's already a quarter to nine—"

". . . And Vakhtang broke his oath. He threw a spear at Baghatar while he was still in the river. The water swept Baghatar's body away, and the Alans and Khazars fled."

The bell rang. I dashed out of the lecture hall before anyone else. Guram followed me. I ran to the courtyard like a madman, then along the street to my house—the first floor, the second, third, fourth . . . My mother, pale-faced, stood at the door.

"What's happened, Mother?"

"They have taken him!" she said.

To prevent myself from falling I sat down on the steps. I stared at Guram, who had come up behind me. Then something pierced my heart and took my breath away.

What would Thavera think now? Oh God! What is happening to me? What will Thavera think of me? What will he think! My temples burned and the blood rushed to my face.

"He isn't here?" Guram asked.

"No!" I said, and stood up.

"Come in the apartment, son!" my mother begged me.

"Yes! Go in," Guram also urged me.

But I didn't hear anything. I began to walk downstairs.

"Don't do that, son!" my mother stood in front of me. Carefully, I moved her aside and continued walking.

"If you love me, don't do it, son," my mother begged me. She ran beside me. The color had gone from her face. I came to Abibo's door and rang the bell. Nobody answered. I pounded my fist on the door—one! two! three! No sound came from inside. I kicked the door.

"Are you crazy?" Guram pulled at my sleeve. I pushed him away and flung my shoulder against the door.

"Come out! Come out! Come out! You scoundrel! Arrest me! I know you're at home! I'll break the door down! Come out, you skunk! Show what kind of a man you are! You wretch! Come out! Arrest me! Come out! Come out!"

"Don't do that, son!" my mother said. The neighbors, hearing the noise, ran out into the hall, and they were all staring at me.

"Come out! Open the door so I can spit in your face!" I spat at the door and began to beat on it with my fist. Then my knees turned to water and I sank down before the door. I put my head on my knees and I began to cry like a child who has been punished unjustly.

Comrade David

———

Teymuraz Baramidze, the sun has been rising and setting twenty-two years for you. It has risen and set for you, as it has for others, for "the sun spreads its light equally on the rose and the dung-pit." Teymuraz Baramidze, you were a carefree and good-natured boy. You loved the sun, the sea and Gulika. You were carefree because you had no responsibilities. You were good, because you were innocent of evil, you loved the sun because it warmed you and did not burn. You loved the sea because it caressed you and did not drown you. You loved Gulika because you missed her always, you could not bear to be without her, and she loved you. You had a friend called Guram, who would

136

never betray you as long as he lived. And now, what have you done with your life, that as you grow older your troubles increase? Why does the sun burn you so fiercely? Why are you afraid of the sea? Why do you no longer desire Gulika? Why do you avoid meeting her? What has happened? Why so many doubts and cares? Wouldn't it be better if man were born a hundred years old, and if with the passing years age and troubles decreased, and sight, hearing and thought gradually faded and you returned to your mother's womb to die untroubled in peace? What footprints will you leave behind you? Whether you walk forward or backward, you will always leave your footprints. Teymuraz Baramidze, what are you thinking about? You don't want to leave behind you the footprints of a man walking in the wrong direction? Then go forward! Are you afraid? What are you afraid of?

I have no fear of anything. Who says I am afraid? Who says the sun burns me, that the sea makes me drown, that I do not love Gulika? Who? Who? Who says that my troubles increase as I grow older?

You! You told me so yourself.

I told you?

Yes, you, Teymuraz Baramidze.

You told me you were afraid of life. But you did not say why. Maybe because you and your mother do not agree with each other? Or maybe because of your meeting in the café with that man Dursun, who let you look into the cave of his dead heart. Or maybe because Abibo spat on your soul. Maybe because nobody believes in Thavera's words. And possibly also because you lost Gulika.

"Gulika, how long has it been since I saw you?"

"How are you, Teymo?"

"What has happened between us, Gulika? We have become so cold to one another?"

"I don't know!"

"Could it be because of what happened by the seaside?"

"I don't think so, Teymo. Probably that was only a pretext."

"A pretext?"

"Yes. Why didn't I want to see you anymore?"

"But we meet every day at the lectures."

"Yes, but we don't meet alone anymore."

"Why, Gulika?"

"I don't know, Teymo. By the name of my mother, I don't know!"

"Have you fallen in love with somebody else?"

"No, Teymo, with nobody. I swear it—with nobody. But I don't miss you. I don't think about you. I don't love you anymore, you have become so strange to me."

"What do you think is so strange about me?"

"The fact that you don't love me anymore in spite of everything you tell me. You are deceiving yourself and me, too."

"Do you think, Gulika, why I don't love you anymore? Why?"

"Probably for the same reason that I don't love you."

"Can you tell me what the reason is?"

"I don't know. Such things have no reasons of their own. Tell me that you don't love me anymore. You are an honest man, aren't you? Then, tell me frankly that you don't love me anymore!"

"I don't love you as I used to."

"You see, I am not asking for the reason."

"Then how must we behave to each other, Gulika?"

"Just as others behave. We must forget everything."

"It is impossible to forget everything."

"It is possible."

"How?"

"Well, I don't remember you. I can't recall your first name."

"My first name is Teymuri."

"Excuse me. I don't remember your last name."

"Teymuri Baramidze. We are in the same class in the School of Economics, in the fourth year."

"I don't know you. I have never met you. Perhaps you don't attend the lectures."

"But I do. I sit behind you on the second bench. Aren't you Gulika Tchibadze, who lives on Lotkin Hill?"

"No, you have me confused with someone else. Excuse me, I must hurry. Good-bye!"

"Good-bye, Gulika!"

"Comrade Baramidze, if possible, please pay attention to what we are saying. It is your problem, not mine, that is being examined by the assembly of the members of the Communist Youth League." The chairman of the assembly rang a bell. The assembly was being held in lecture hall number 90. Fifty students were present, and in addition there were Comrade David, the secretary of the faculty Party Committee, and Comrade Guiorgui, the lecturer on law.

On the agenda for discussion was a single item: the excesses of student Baramidze, who staged a drunken brawl and committed a physical offense, namely, breaking the door of a neighbor and grievously insulting a reponsible worker, calling him a beggar, although the above-mentioned worker has never been known to engage in such activity.

I was sitting near the wall on the bench reserved for the accused.

Absorbed in my own thoughts, I had not heard the indictment read by the secretary of the committee, Ushangui Khochakidze.

Probably it was because of this that the chairman rebuked me.

"Comrades," continued the secretary, "this case shows that the politico-educational work of our faculty leaves much to be desired. Indeed, it is lame in both legs. At the next meeting of the committee we shall bring this question up for discussion. Comrades, we have had enough! Enough of this infamy, this shame! Who avoids going to lectures? Baramidze and Tchitchinadze! Who must take a second examination? Baramidze and Tchitchinadze! Who has failed to pay his membership fee? Baramidze and Tchitchinadze!"

"I would give my life for our faithful Ushangui, but I don't think it is my problem which is being investigated today!" Guram jumped to his feet.

"Comrade Tchitchinadze, your turn will come soon!" Ushangui shouted.

"Please discuss my problem at the same time."

"Comrade Tchitchinadze, you must not tell me when to speak!" Ushangui said, and he looked at the chairman. The chairman rang his bell. Guram sat down.

"Comrade Baramidze, explain to the assembly the reason for your hooliganism!" Ushangui said.

"I don't remember anything, I was very drunk!" I replied.

"Then you do not deny that you were very drunk?" the chairman said.

"No."

Guram stood up. "He is lying! I was there at the time, and Teymo was not drunk!"

"Meaning that Tchitchinadze declares the act of violence took place at a time when the accused was sober."

"I did not say that. I said only that Teymo was not drunk."

"Comrade Baramidze, what would you say about Tchitchinadze's declaration?"

"Haven't I told you that I don't remember anything?"

"What were your intentions when you tried to break down the door and used bad language to your neighbor, who, as we have already mentioned, is a responsible person."

"He probably had some good reasons and that is why he was cursing," Guram said.

"What reason did you have, Baramidze?"

"I don't remember!"

"Maybe you remember, Tchitchinadze, or perhaps you were also drunk?"

"Brother, you will have to speak to me decently, otherwise, if I get hold of you, I'll beat you so unmercifully that even a responsible person won't recognize you!"

"Comrade Tchitchinadze, your insolence will be noted in the committee's minutes!"

"Note anything you like, but if you are our comrade, then talk to us like a comrade. If you think that by deepening your voice so that you sound like a man with tonsillitis—'What were your intentions when . . . ?'" Guram imitated the voice. Ushangui interrupted him. "This is an official assembly, Tchitchinadze, and everything has to be done according to the rules."

"If this is an official assembly, then let the responsible person attend our meeting!"

"That is not your business, Comrade Tchitchinadze. The chairman of the assembly knows his duties," said Ushangui, and he looked at the chairman. The chairman nodded.

"Tell us, Baramidze, what was your explanation?"

"I haven't one."

"Nothing?"

"In any case I won't tell you!"

"Then tell the assembly."

"The assembly would not be interested. Lots of things happen among neighbors."

"That is, you will not obey the assembly. Do you know what the penalty is? You could be excluded from the Young Communist League!"

"You can exclude only those you yourself have admitted. I was accepted by the general assembly!"

"Enough, comrades!" Ushangui went on. "It is time to put an end to these abominations! Who took part in a drunken brawl? Baramidze! Who offended the responsible person? Baramidze!"

"Who is this responsible person? Show him to us. Has he no first or last name? What is wrong with him that even his name must not be mentioned?" asked Agrafena Danelya.

"Don't meddle in affairs that don't concern you, Comrade Danelya!" The chairman rang the bell.

"Comrade Chairman, if it is not our affair, then why did you summon us? We might as well get up and go!" Agrafena was hurt.

"You will go when we tell you to go. It is bad enough that you have come here wearing earrings and makeup. Where do you think you are?"

"Comrade Chairman, what does it matter to you whether Agrafena walks around with earrings and makeup on her face or with jam on her lips?" asked Archil.

"Are we building Communism or not, Comrade Archil?" Ushangui said.

"I don't know about you, but I am."

"Do you mean to tell me that I am not building Communism?" Ushangui asked in great astonishment.

"I don't know, I work in another department," said Archil, avoiding an answer.

"I ask you, what right have you to intercede for a woman who is dressed in a skirt so short that it shows two inches of her legs above her knees?"

There was a general commotion in the lecture hall. Everyone looked at Agrafena. Agrafena became red as a beet and her eyes filled with tears.

I told Ushangui it was time to talk about me. "Let them discuss me, Comrade Chairman. Submit Agrafena's short skirt for discussion at the next assembly together with any problems concerning Tchitchinadze."

Ushangui pointed at me with his index finger. "Don't you see, comrades, how he hurls derision among the assembly and considers himself absolutely innocent!"

"You yourself are deriding the assembly," Guram said. "We are here to discuss a serious matter and you talk about short skirts and earrings!"

"Comrade Tchitchinadze, you are greatly mistaken if you think that short skirts, earrings and makeup are not serious problems. All this is just as important as . . ." Ushangui paused, but could not remember what he intended to say.

"As important as what?" Guram asked.

"As important as . . ."

Again Ushangui could not remember. "And don't overlook the fact that we cannot permit people wearing short skirts, makeup and earrings to enter our Communist society."

"So you stand sentry at the door," Archil said.

"And what I have said is also true about narrow pants," Ushangui said.

"Therefore you will stand at the door, and only unwashed people with disheveled hair, and without makeup, and without earrings, with long skirts and wide pants are allowed to enter?" The audience laughed. The chairman rang the bell.

"Comrade Archil, you will have the floor later!"

"We shall submit a complaint against you at the next assembly for your insolence!" Ushangui went on, thus adding another subject to be discussed at the next meeting.

"Then submit it, submit it, and don't forget about it!" Archil shouted.

Loud protests ran like a wind through the audience.

The bad-tempered Liuba jumped to her feet, saying explosively, "Does this mean we are not allowed to be well-dressed and in the proper style?"

"Comrade Liuba, you and Agrafena are both stu-

dents. It has been observed that you always make
up your eyebrows and during lectures you wear a ring
on the middle finger of your left hand. And on top
of that, your very red nail polish only adds to your
disgrace. In your place, I would keep my mouth
shut!" Ushangui advised her.

"I am not your comrade, you idiot! I am a married woman and it is my affair if I want to wear a
ring, make up my eyebrows or shave off my hair.
I don't have to ask you, you contemptible creature!"
Liuba screamed at him.

"Comrade Liuba, for your personal offense a complaint against you will be submitted at the next
meeting!" the chairman shouted back at her.

Liuba began to cry, and leaned against the bench.
The audience became enraged.

"Come down from the podium!"

"You really think you can teach us sense, but you
are all nitwits!"

"Come here, Teymo. Come and sit with us!"

"So you think it is of no importance that you and
Ilo have embezzled the funds of the professional
union? You'd better look to your own business!"

"Who said that?" Ushangui asked, purple with
rage.

"I did!" said Othar Saneblidze, and he stood up.

"By what right?"

"I know the facts."

"How do you know them?"

"Ilo told me himself!" Ushangui's jaw dropped,
and everyone in the hall roared.

"I shall not let this accusation pass. At the next
meeting . . ." Someone whistled. Suddenly Comrade
David stood up and asked for the floor. The audience
fell silent. "Comrades," he began. "It is very sad that
such a situation has been created. It appears that
the committee of the Communist League had not prepared for and had not even studied the question of
Baramidze before placing it on the agenda. Com-

rade Ushangui, that is not the way it should be done. I do not know to what extent Baramidze is guilty or innocent, but the fact is that there does not exist even the minimum of mutual understanding among you, or respect. Comrade Guiorgui, I call upon you to answer the question whether it is possible under these conditions to continue the assembly's discussions?" he said, addressing the lecturer.

Comrade Guiorgui stood up. He looked at the audience with eyes full of reproach, then shook his head sadly and removed his glasses.

"To speak truthfully, we are admirers of discipline, severe discipline. Probably, this is the result of frequent close contact with students during our scientific activity over a long period of time. We may say that reciprocal comparisons and analyses made over many years, as well as the intellectual interpretation of the present stage in the development of events—I am referring to the appreciation of the coordination of disciplines—indicate a terrible dissonance, a lowering of the pulse, a casuistry, that is, a breakdown of moral-aesthetic norms. The word 'student,' as a concept, is now synonymous with absolute frustration or moral disintegration. Who is a hooligan? A student. Who is a brigand? A student. Who is rude? A student. Whenever some offense is reported in the Agriculture Department or some other branch, who is found to be guilty? A student. I have educated thousands and thousands of students, comrades!"

"Have you read *The Tutor* by Akaki Tsereteli,[1] Mr. Guiorgui?" Mr. David asked. The audience exploded in Homeric laughter.

"I understood your allusion, Comrade David, but you must know that I have read Diderot, Rousseau, Voltaire, Machiavelli, Napoleon, and Bismarck's memoirs. It pains me to contemplate the fate of our

---

[1] This "Georgian Pushkin" after hearing his student confess to a crime, committed suicide because he felt responsible for his student's up-bringing.

young generation, and because of this I speak so
severely. I liked our speaker's address, even though
it was somewhat intemperate. His observations are
basically right. The next generation must be our hope.
But who will inherit this country, built at the cost
of so much blood and suffering? These people? The
generation prancing around in narrow pants and
pointed shoes? The future mothers of Georgia with
plucked eyebrows, rouged faces and short skirts?"

"My dear fellow, Alexander of Macedon walked
around totally naked and yet he conquered the whole
world. As for eyebrows, even the great Queen Thamar
used to pluck hers, and they say she also put rouge
on her face," Comrade David said.

The audience laughed heartily.

"This is not an exercise in polemics, Comrade
David. By your leave, may I continue? In my youth,
when we were building this country, I held my
Mauser in one hand and a book in the other." Comrade Guiorgui suddenly became excited.

"I was not aware of that, my dear Guiorgui. As
I look at you, it seems to me it would have been
better if you had held books in both hands!" Comrade David smiled at him.

Comrade Guiorgui was taken aback.

"You defend this youth who has no education,
no honesty, no decency, does not know anything about
discipline, and has no respect for age. Do you know
that the companion of this youth here, a student,
yesterday killed a man in Kirov Park? Do you know
that a week ago their companions, two students,
robbed a store? That a friend of this man," Mr.
Guiorgui pointed to me, "raped a woman in Kukia
cemetery, and that another of their friends, a girl
student, gave birth to an illegitimate child?" Comrade Guiorgui struck the table with his hand.

"Do you know," Comrade David replied, "that a
companion of this youth covered a gun port with
his body? Do you know that to protect her friend, a

girl student went to the gallows? Do you know that
yesterday his friend saved a man your age from
drowning in Mtkvari? You do not know, you do not
even want to know, and it is not obligatory for you
to know!"

Comrade David was interrupted by the thunder of
loud and prolonged applause.

"I do not know what offense Baramidze has committed," Comrade David went on, "but it is very easy
to find out, and probably the Party Buro or the Rector's Office will bring it to light today or tomorrow,
because Comrade Ushangui Khochakidze has shown
no competence in his task. And if Baramidze deserves punishment, he will be punished. But now
I am troubled by another matter. Why this vehemence
against youth? What right do you have to accuse the
audience, your schoolmates, your friends, in such a
drastic way? How do you know exactly how many
inches above her knees Comrade Danelya wears her
skirt? Who measures the skirts? Who prescribes the
rule about their length? How do you happen to know
about her skirt?"

"When she was drinking at the water fountain, she
leaned over and I could see her naked body!"
Ushangui yelped.

"Then why were you looking, you prude? Shall
Comrade Danelya drink no water for fear that you
might be looking?"

"It was quite involuntary."

"That is, you couldn't take your eyes off her?"
Comrade David said, and the whole audience was
laughing.

"What concern is it of yours, Comrade Ushangui,
whether Liuba Nodia paints her nails? Who authorized
you to rule on whether Archil's pants should be narrow or not? I'd rather have one of his poems than
you and your broad trousers!"

"This world does not depend on you!" exclaimed
Ushangui.

"And neither does it depend on you, my friend Ushangui! Who appointed you to watch at the gates of Communism? Who authorized you to measure the skirts and trousers of the people entering Communism? It is a moot point whether you yourself should be allowed to enter the world of Communism. And, Comrade Guiorgui, who gave you the right to come here and besmirch the name of our vigorous youth! Youth will come into its own and inherit this world and so it has happened with every past generation. Youth will bury us and on our gravestones they will inscribe our first and last names."

"Comrade David, you are provoking us!" Guiorgui shouted.

Comrade David did not pay any attention to him and went on:

"Our youth is indeed our hope. Let our youth wear narrow and short skirts, as they please. Only let them read books, let them love the nation, their native country, the world. Let the girls wear earrings and finger rings, only let them be good mothers and believe in goodness and honesty as people used to believe in God. Let Baramidze fight, but let him fight only for what is noble. And if someone has killed a man, or someone has robbed a store, that is not a national tragedy."

Comrade David ended his speech. His lips and hands were trembling.

"Excuse me," he said. "The discussion is now over."

Except for Guiorgui and Ushangui, nobody moved.

I am sitting in the Rector's waiting room. I have an appointment for one o'clock. It is only twelve, but I am sitting there and waiting. Some other students are also waiting. They go in and come out, go in and come out. Some come out cheerful, others weeping. The Rector is a severe man, very severe. To tell the truth, I have never had anything to do with him. I have never experienced either his severity or his

goodness, but it is said that he is very stern and because of that my heart feels faint. During four years
this man has threatened me as my mother used to
threaten me in my childhood by calling on the yard-
keeper, Mameda.

It is very strange. Mameda had seven children and
not one of them feared him. But I never dared to
go into the yard for fear of him. It was not only me,
but all the other children, at the mere appearance of
Mameda in the yard, ran screaming and shrieking
upstairs. Mameda always seemed astonished by it.

"Our child is scared to death by this monster.
Couldn't they send him to the other house?" my
Aunt Martha said.

"It is because of him that my Datho stammers,"
my Uncle Petre said, stroking Datho's head. "He has
probably been scared out of his wits!"

In the evening I sat in my mother's lap. On the
table there is a huge plate, full of rice broth, and
my mother presses a spoonful of broth against my
teeth.

"Open your mouth, otherwise I shall call Mameda
and he will put you in his sack . . ." I am so
frightened that I open my mouth.

"One more, or else I'll tell Mameda and tomorrow
he'll sell you in the market . . ."

"One more, or else Mameda will put you in the
dustbin . . ."

"Haven't you swallowed it yet? I'll call for Mameda to take you to the police station. Mameda,
Mameda, come here! Teymo doesn't want to eat!"

"I'll eat! I'll eat!" I shouted and thrust the spoon
into my mouth right up to the handle. After that I
dreamed all night about Mameda with his sack,
squeezing me and putting me inside as though I
were a corn tassel. He tied up his sack and took me
away. It was dark in the sack. I was swaying on
Mameda's back as though in a hammock. Mameda
had a big soft stride. Mameda walked for a long

time, and then stopped abruptly, turned around,
swung the sack and put it down. I fell down and
down, something was buzzing in my ears.

"Help me! Help me!" I screamed. The sack opened
and I put out my head. Below me there was a huge
steep rock, and there was a tree on the rock. If I
could catch on to this tree while I fell, I would be
saved. But if I went past it, then there was only an
enormous sea below and I would be drowned in it.

"Help! Help!" I screamed, as I fell into the foaming sea. Soon I would be drowned. But I was breathing in the sea. The sea was very warm, blue and
transparent. I saw everything in the sea. I breathed,
and little by little I sank down. I walked on the
bottom of the sea, I swam, I hung upside down,
lay on my back, lay on my belly, I breathed and
breathed and blew bubbles. Then I sat down on a
big mossy stone, took a pipe from my shirt, and
played a very sad song:

The fortress of Surami,which I long to see,
My son is there, keep him well . . .

An old beggar in Surami used to sing that song.
It always made my mother cry. I would cry too.
Then my mother would give me some coins. I would
throw them into the beggar's greasy hat, and it always surprised me that the beggar did not weep.

I played on the pipe. The little fishes, gold, silver,
green, red and blue, came toward me. They surrounded me and were spellbound, faintly wagging
their tails, blowing bubbles, and crying; then they
blew more bubbles and said:

"Why are you crying, little boy?"

"My golden fishes, my silver fishes, my green
fishes . . . go and tell my mother that I am here, and
I am not drowned, and I can breathe in the water
and I am well, only I miss my mother. Tell her to
come and get me."

"What is your mother's name, little boy?" the fishes said.

"My mother's name is Anika!"

"How can we find your mother?"

"My mother is the best, the sweetest, the prettiest mother in the whole world. When you see her, you will recognize her at once. My golden fishes, my silver fishes . . ."

"Very well, we'll find her, but you must play for us once more."

So I play:

The fortress of Surami, which I long to see,
My son is there, keep him well . . .

The fishes swam away. They disappeared gradually and I was alone, playing on my pipe and weeping. Then, quite suddenly, I saw my mother swimming toward me with outstretched hands. My mother swam surrounded by the gold, silver, red, green and blue fishes and my mother is the prettiest among these fishes.

"Mother!" I cried and swam to meet her.

I awoke in the morning. My mother clothed me, fed me and let me go out in the yard to play. In the yard there is a big acacia tree, the branches nearly reaching into our window. I removed my shoes, and at the same time looked up to be sure my mother could not see me. I climbed up and picked some acacia blossoms, and then stuffed them under my shirt. Then I climbed down, and sat in the shed built onto the stone house near Mameda's broom. I filled my mouth with the flowers. Acacia blossoms are as sweet as honey. When I have finished eating them, then I will climb up again, and fill my mouth again.

"What are you doing here, boy? Are you mad?" I heard the voice of Mameda. My hands and feet were frozen. I wanted to howl, but my mouth was full of acacia blossoms.

"Throw them away at once, or I'll come and cut off your ears! If you swallow one little ant, your stomach will swell up like a drum! Throw them away at once!"

Mameda took my chin in his hand and opened my mouth. I ejected the half-chewed blossoms into the palm of his hand.

"Ai, ai, what a bad thing for a good boy to do!" Mameda shook his head.

"You won't put me into your sack?" I said, frightened.

"Where is my sack?" Mameda said.

"You won't put me into the dustbin?" I repeated, full of fear.

"There is so little garbage, and how could I put a golden boy like you into the dustbin?" Mameda was smiling.

"You won't call a policeman?" I said, not trusting him.

"I will call a policeman if you eat any more acacia!" Mameda threatened me.

"I'll never eat any more, Uncle Mameda!" I promised.

"Very well. If you're hungry, you may have some bread and cheese," Mameda said.

Then he went into his cellar, called his wife and said something in the Kurdish language. Mameda's wife brought some black bread and cheese, and he took it and gave it to me.

"Eat it," he said, and I took the black bread and cheese, and all the while his dog was staring at me.

I ate with a great appetite.

"Teymuri, what are you eating? Throw it away immediately and come up to the house!" my mother called from the balcony.

"I am coming!" I shouted, but I did not go to her.

"Which is Baramidze?" the Rector's secretary Thina asked from the open door.

"I am!" I said, and stood up. Nearsighted Thina squinted at me, her eyes squinting still more as though she wanted to check on whether I was really Baramidze. Then she said, "Go in," in a voice implying that I had been begging her to do this favor for me for at least a month. I opened the door carefully and closed it behind me. Two men were sitting at the huge desk, the secretary of our faculty Party Buro and the Rector. It was the first time in my life I had been in such a large, clean, and well-furnished study, and I had never seen the Rector so close to me. I felt weak in my knees, sweat moistened the palms of my hands, and I was unable to take a single step forward.

The Rector stood up. He was very tall, bald, and his bushy eyebrows gave his stern face an even more severe expression.

"This is Baramidze!" Comrade David said to the Rector, and smiled.

"Sit down!" the Rector said to me, pointing to a large leather armchair. I did not move.

"Sit down, Baramidze!" Comrade David repeated.

"Excuse me, I will remain standing!" I said.

"Didn't you hear me? Come here and sit down!" the Rector commanded. I went up to the table.

"How are you?"

"How do you do!" the Rector said and he stretched out his hand. I wiped my sweaty palm on my hip and only then stretched it out to him. The Rector smiled.

"He is a peasant!" he said to the Party representative. I sat down. The Rector sat down, too. There was silence. The Rector took a huge red pencil and began to draw something in a notebook.

"What is your name?" he asked me.

"Teymuraz," I said and stood up.

"Sit down," he motioned me with his hand and continued to draw on his notebook.

The Party representative was looking at a newspaper and did not utter a word.

I was sure they intended to do something to me, and the Party Buro would also do something to me, but what it would be I could not guess. So we were silent for a long time, all three of us. As the time dragged on, I began to feel ill. My heart felt congested and almost faint. I wanted to stand up and could not. My mouth was so dry that I could not move my tongue. With my eyes I followed the huge copper pendulum of the clock as it moved from right to left, left to right. Everything looked multi-colored, everything around me began to whirl and to be confused. Probably ten minutes passed or fifteen, or an hour or more. If only I could have some of that water there in the pink pitcher. O God, how happy I would be if the Rector would only pour some water into a glass and offer me a drink. But if he did not, I told myself I would go mad, I would faint and go mad! Whatever happens I must get up and get myself a drink, they can do whatever they wish with me, I don't care, but I must have a drink. But what if they deny me the water, what then? No, I cannot stand it anymore, I will now stand up and pour the water, I will empty the whole pitcher! I will drink directly from the pitcher.

"Honorable Rector!" I stood up.

"Yes?" He lifted his head.

"May I have a drink of water?"

"Please," the Rector said, and continued to draw on his notebook. I poured one glass, drank it, and drank a second glass.

"Please leave a little for us!" the Rector said. I put the glass on the table and took a long breath.

"Is there no water where you live?" he said.

"Yes, sir!" I said.

"Now tell us how it happened?" he went on, preparing to listen to me.

"Sir, I had nothing to do with it!"

"Do you know what I am talking about?"

I was baffled. "You are asking about the assembly meeting?" I answered, and looked at the Party representative.

"Comrade David has told me all about the assembly meeting. I will speak about that separately with the faculty. Now tell us about your drunken attack on your neighbor," the Rector said, frowning.

He resembled an eagle sitting on a mountain summit, about to fly away. It is no use, I could never fool him, it would be better to tell the whole truth. Probably he knows it already. Abibo called all the authorities on the telephone, and he must certainly have called the Rector, too. If they wish to expel me, they can do that without my confession, and if not . . . It is better to tell the truth, maybe they will believe me, maybe he will understand, and if he did understand . . . but it is impossible that this man should not understand me.

"Honorable Rector, I swear by my mother that I was not drunk," I began.

"Don't you drink wine?" the Rector said.

"Yes, but at the time I was not drunk."

"The worse for you!" the Rector said. "So it was a deliberate attack?"

"Yes, I did it deliberately!"

"Why?"

"One week ago, Honorable Rector, some prisoners escaped. Two were killed, three got away. Among these three one was my friend, my schoolmate." My voice began to tremble.

"That friend, a thief, was taken from your house, Baramidze!" the Rector said and frowned again.

"Yes, from my house. Nobody knew about his being with me, only I, my mother and Abibo."

"Abibo Thodria works in the N.K.V.D., he is a re-

sponsible person, and he would have to report it!"
the Rector interrupted. My heart was wrung. I was
finished, I should not have told him. I should have
known he would not understand anything. And how
could he understand, if he maintained that Abibo was
obliged to report it. I will tell him nothing more.
It is all over. I stopped speaking.

"What happened then, Teymuraz?" Comrade David
asked me. I was sitting with bent head, saying nothing. The Rector stood up, walked to the middle of
the room and began to smoke, then he came up to
me and said:

"Tell me, only tell me the whole truth."

I said nothing.

"Baramidze, Comrade David spoke to me about
you, and I don't want to take any measures without
knowing everything," the Rector said.

"Teymuri, we are trying to help you, and you must
collaborate with us," Comrade David said.

"I don't need help," I said. "I will tell the whole
truth. I had not seen Thavera for six years. Then he
ran away from prison and came to me. He does not
want to steal anymore, he wishes to study. Abibo is
a dishonest man. He is a filthy swine! I want to kill
him!" I could not breathe, and I stood up. The
Rector and Comrade David looked at me, astonished.

"Sit down and tell us exactly what happened." The
Rector put his hand on my shoulder. I sat down.

"Thavera wrote a thousand declarations begging
forgiveness, saying he would never steal again, he
was exhausted, he wished to study, to work. He wrote
a thousand letters which nobody read. Nobody believed him, nobody trusted him, so he ran away.
He came to me, asked me for help."

"And then, Teymuraz," Comrade David asked me.

"Then," I began, "well, I did not know anyone
except Abibo. I came to him, knelt before him and
asked him to believe in Thavera, because if you will
not believe him, he will steal again, he will perish or

commit suicide. I knelt before him, begged him, and
he promised to help and instead he had Thavera
arrested. Then I went to Abibo's apartment, but he
was not there, or, if he was there, he did not open
the door. Doesn't that show that he was a dishonest
and dishonorable man, and deserves to be killed?"
I said and fell silent.

The Rector sat with bent head for a long time,
drawing something. No, he was not drawing anymore, but with fast movements of his pencil he was
retouching his drawing.

"Do you believe in Thavera?" the Rector asked
me suddenly, and looked straight into my eyes.

"I do believe him!" I said.

"Does he want to study?"

"He does!"

"How many years does he have to serve in prison?"

"Four years, and in four years his life could come
to an end."

"In four years a man's life does not come to an
end."

"For Thavera it would be the end, Honorable
Rector!"

"What is the last name of Thavera?"

"Korsaveli. His name is not really Thavera, but
Ramaz. Thavera is his nickname."

"Ramaz Korsaveli, Ramaz Korsaveli." For some reason the Rector repeated the name.

"In which class are you?" he went on.

"In the fourth class."

"Does he study well?" the Rector now asked Comrade David.

"He studies," said Comrade David and smiled.

"What kind of person is he?"

"Such as you see."

"It is good to like your friends and believe in them,
but it is not possible to believe in everybody." The
Rector turned to me.

"It is possible to trust Thavera!" I said.

"If your Thavera really wants to study, he could have endured four years more and not run away. Running away from prison is a serious crime, do you know that?"

"I do!"

"Go away now. Stay with your friends, keep out of mischief, study well, and mind your own business. Thavera will arrange his affairs for himself."

The Rector stood up, so did I and Comrade David. I looked at the Rector's notebook. He had drawn a lovely, lopeared, naive donkey, red, with hanging head and sad eyes. Under the donkey, in the same red pencil, was written—*Ramaz Korsaveli (Thavera)*. In the far corner, in large characters totally incomprehensible to me, were three figures—233.

"Good-bye!" I said.

"Good-bye!" the Rector said.

I went to the door. Comrade David followed me.

"David, stay here!" the Rector said. Comrade David sat down. I closed the door behind me.

"What kind of a mood is he in?" a student ran to ask me.

"Don't go in! He will kill you!" I said and went out.

I went down to the courtyard and sat in a chair under a weeping mulberry tree.

From afar the university resembles a beehive. Around its doors the bees buzz steadily, the workers and the drones: they enter and leave in a continuous stream, in and out through the carved doors, where the guards stand with armbands on their sleeves. They zealously check the passes of everyone entering the university. Whoever has a pass is allowed to enter, whoever does not have one is turned away, like a drone bee. Commotion and uproar reign day and night, night and day.

Professors, like queen bees, are treated with more respect. When they appear, the guards bow their heads down to the earth. The professors, in their turn, respectfully remove their hats, and with bent heads, they enter through the doors, which are flung wide open for them, as though they were entering a temple.

The university, with its many libraries, auditoriums, benches, chairs and rostrums, its standing guards and buzzing students, is amazingly like a beehive. It is a hive—a hive for dragons—no, not dragons, but gods! A hive overflowing with honey—and what a joy it is to know that you, too, live in this beehive in the service of the gods.

Galaktioni

Someone sat down beside me and put his hand on my knee. I looked up—it was Guram.

"Teymo, what are you thinking of, now?"

"Nothing."

"What happened?"

"I saw the Rector. I was summoned because of the assembly and Abibo."

"Did he understand?"

"Everything."

"Then?"

"I told him everything. I told him the whole truth."

"What did he say?"

"Go and mind your own business, don't let it happen again. He wrote down the first and last name of Thavera."

"What for?"

"I don't know."

"Let's go sit somewhere else, where you can tell me everything," he said. I stood up. All the tables were occupied in the Intourist garden, so Guram and I sat down at the table beside the fountain. We ordered beer before receiving our food. The waiter brought two bottles of cold beer. I sprinkled salt on the edge of the glass and began to drink slowly. A pleasant coolness ran through my whole body. To the right of us in the corner sat a man with his back to us. He had very broad, somewhat bent shoulders. He was drinking wine. He looked very familiar. Suddenly he banged on a plate with his fork, turned toward us and addressed the waiter:

"Brother, how long do I have to wait?"

"I'm coming!" the waiter shouted. "I can't grow wings, there are millions like you and I am alone!" The waiter seemed rather hurt, and as he waited for our order to be prepared, his pencil hovered over his pad.

"Guram, look!"

"Who?"

"Galaktioni!"

Guram turned round immediately. Galaktioni was sitting with his back to us.

"Wait on him first," I told the waiter.

"Give me your order and I'll bring his, too," the waiter said, grinning. "That fellow has been sitting and staring at a bottle of wine for two hours." I gave the order and asked the waiter to take everything to Galaktioni's table.

"Go and talk to him, Guram!"

"Won't he be offended?"

"Why should he be offended? Go and talk to him!"

Guram agreed and we stood up. When we were

standing in front of him, Galaktioni looked at us with amazement.

"May we sit at your table, sir?" I said. Galaktioni looked around the restaurant, and seeing so many free tables, he laughed.

"There are plenty of other tables in this restaurant."

"But we want to be with you!" Guram said in such a way that not only Galaktioni but even I was moved.

"Of course, of course, sit down!" Galaktioni said, and we sat with him. There was an uneasy silence.

"Well, who are you?" Galaktioni said, breaking the silence.

"We are students, Mr. Galaktioni."

"So you are studying?"

"We are."

"Good, wonderful, remarkable!" he said, and took the bottle in his hand. Suddenly he became agitated, began to search for something, then stood up and from the neighboring table brought two glasses and put them before me and Guram.

"Do you drink wine?"

"We do."

"You know me, don't you?" he asked and began to pour the wine.

"Who does not know you, Mr. Galaktioni?" Guram said.

"The waiter does not recognize me. He has been looking at me for a whole hour and he simply does not recognize me." Galaktioni laughed. The waiter came, brought three bottles of wine, some cheese, some boiled dry meat and salad.

"Do you recognize me, brother?" Galaktioni asked the waiter.

"Of course I recognize you. Don't you come here every day?" the waiter smiled at him.

"Then tell me, what do I look like?"

"Like a priest," the waiter said, gazing at Galaktioni's beard.

"Quite right, brother. I resemble a priest as you resemble a donkey." Galaktioni roared with laughter.

"So you call me a donkey just because I am waiting on you?" The waiter was hurt.

"No, brother, you're like a donkey because you don't wait on me!"

The waiter went off with a cold look on his face. Galaktioni continued to laugh.

"Didn't I tell you he doesn't recognize me!" he said at last, after he finished laughing. "Now, you tell me, who do I resemble?"

Shivers ran through my whole body. What on earth could I say?

"Are you laughing at us, Mr. Galaktioni?" Guram said in the voice of a dying man.

"No, brother, I am asking the question quite seriously."

"You are like nobody else, Mr. Galaktioni. You are Galaktioni, the great poet Galaktioni Tabidze.[1] Who could be like you?" I said.

"True, I am Galaktioni Tabidze, but who do I look like?"

"Goethe!" Guram said.

"No!"

"Rusthaveli, Firdausi . . ."

"No, no, brother, I am like Akaki Tsereteli, surely?" he said, passing his hand over his beard.

"Of course, there is a resemblance, a great resemblance, sir!" I said.

"You see, everybody tells me that I am like Akaki, only the waiter could not recognize me. Long live Akaki!" Galaktioni said and he emptied his glass. We also emptied our glasses.

Galaktioni was a little drunk already. In his wonderfully deep, clever and smiling eyes there was a

---

[1] Galaktioni Tabidze (1892–1962) was in fact a Georgian poet of considerable eminence, much loved by the people. He committed suicide in 1962.

mischievous spark. He became cheerful and garru-
lous.

"What do you do, brothers? Do you not write
poems?"

"I don't, but he does!" Guram said.

"I don't write poems anymore!"

"Why, brother, everybody writes and what harm is
there in it? Write, write! It is good to write poems,"
Galaktioni said and patted my head.

"To write such poems as you write is very good,
Mr. Galaktioni!" I answered.

"It is good to write bad poems too. It is not necessary that everyone writes good poems." Galaktioni
laughed, and I noticed that he was playing with us
as a soccer-player plays with the ball. Guram listened
with open mouth. I wanted to cover his mouth, so
that he should not blurt out some triviality, but I
was too late.

"How do you write your poems, Mr. Galaktioni?"
he blurted out, and looked triumphantly in my direction.

Galaktioni looked at Guram in such a way that my
heart ached with pity for him. Then he poured some
more wine, took a little piece of meat and put in on
the edge of his plate. He closed his eyes.

"I love the sea very much, the sea and the sun.
Every summer I go to the sea. I have a house in
Sukhumi, as you know," he said and opened his
eyes. We nodded. Galaktioni again closed his eyes and
went on: "I go to Sukhumi every summer, dig a great
hole in the sand, and lie in it. The sand covers me up
to the neck. Then I look into the face of the sun,
like this, as I am doing now. At first it is dark, then
there appear red, yellow and orange rings, and then
a great, splendid sun enters the eyes. The sun penetrates my eyelids, bones, flesh and blood. The sun
penetrates everything, even the grave. Then there descends from the sky a white angel, a pretty, white
angel, who comes down to my ear and dictates to

me . . ." Galaktioni fell silent. He sat still for a long time, his eyes closed, and I thought that at this very moment he could see the white angel near his ear, dictating his poems, huge and shining like the sun. Then he opened his eyes and I swear I saw in his eyes two huge, burning suns.

"So it is, brother," he said very seriously and raised his glass. "Long live the angel!" Then he drank some more wine.

"Mr. Galaktioni, does the angel really dictate the poems to you?" I said timidly.

"Yes, brother, the angel does indeed dictate. How else would I have time to write poems?" he said, as though feeling sorry for himself.

"*Nikortsmenda* too? Did the angel dictate that to you?"

"Yes, the angel dictated *Nikortsmenda*," Galaktioni nodded. Silence.

"Where is our waiter, why doesn't he come?" Galaktioni said, suddenly becoming anxious.

I banged a fork against a plate. On the left side of the restaurant there was a great commotion. Some people had pushed four tables together and all the waiters in the restaurant were waiting on them. Our waiter was among them.

"Why don't you come here?" I waved my hand at him. He spread out his hands and ran to the kitchen.

"He will come in a moment, Mr. Galaktioni," I said.

"The long-lost beloved will arrive, but when . . . ?" Galaktioni said playfully.

After a while, the waiter came to our table.

"Where have you been, brother? You are starving us to death!" Guram said angrily.

"How do you expect me to serve you? Don't you see who is visiting us?" The waiter was surprised.

"Who?" Guram asked.

"The champion wrestler of the world!"

"What is his name?"

"Haven't you heard about Kithuashvili Goguia? Don't you read the newspapers?" The waiter was angry with Guram. "The doctors said he had the strength of two three-year-old bullocks," the waiter went on, and then he dashed away.

At the head of the joined tables, surrounded by a circle of enthusiastic waiters and sightseers, sat the possessor of the strength of two bullocks, Kithuash-vili Goguia, who was crushing the bones of a boiled shoulder-blade with his powerful jaws.

"I'm going now, my children. Thank you very, very much. Good-bye, good-bye," Galaktioni said, standing up.

"We will accompany you, Mr. Galaktioni," we said, jumping up.

"No, no, why should you accompany me?"

He walked with slow steps. The godlike poet walked through the whole restaurant unnoticed. Once more I was sorry for the divinity in him, so close to humanity, so human, so touching and so simple, that nobody believed in his divinity. Galaktioni passed through the restaurant and crossed the street.

At the head of the joined tables, holding a bowl in his hand, the toastmaster delivered a toast to the man who had brought the name of little Georgia to international attention, who had made our name re-sound through the whole world, who could lift a dumbbell weighing sixty pounds three hundred times in succession, who could twist an iron pipe the size of his wrist around his arm, who could bend a steel bar over his knee and with his head break the trunk of an oak tree, who had defeated eight other wrestlers in a single city, who had never received a penalty and who now, surrounded by glory, had returned peacefully to his native land. The grateful Georgian people wished him health and long life and hoped he would never compromise the splendor of our country.

"Brothers and friends," the toastmaster said. "I call on you to stand up and drink a toast to our knight,

who has done so much for Georgia that if each of
us should live for a hundred years, he would not
achieve even half as much!" Everyone in the restaurant stood up. Guram took a bottle and struck the
plate with all the force he had. The plate shattered
like salt. Everyone turned to look at us.

"What's the matter?"

The waiter ran over to us.

"Nothing. I broke the plate. The check, please,"
said Guram.

"One hundred and fifty-six rubles, including the
plate," the waiter said. We paid. The waiter dashed
off to the table of the great wrestler. We went out.
At the door I looked back. The toastmaster was hanging on the neck of the champion and kissing his
cheeks. Until we reached Khasvethe we didn't say a
word.

"The man is doing his job, a good job. He is a
champion, God help him. He really deserves our gratitude. So why did you abuse him?" I asked Guram.

"I have nothing against him!" Guram said and
laughed bitterly.

"These idiots deserve to be killed, the toastmaster,
the waiters, all of them!"

"I have nothing against them either!" Guram said,
shrugging his shoulders and slipping his arm through
mine.

Kirov Park

————

I have never been in Hyde Park, but I doubt if, even there, one could hear as many sensational, amusing, fantastic stories and rumors as in our Kirov Park. It was in Kirov Park that I heard for the first time that the Prime Minister of Persia, Mossadegh, was a swindler, that Churchill drinks three bottles of cognac a day, that Truman poisoned Roosevelt, that Harriman studied in the gymnasium of Kutaisi until he was fourteen years old, and that Boria Paichadze wore gold boots when he played soccer against the Basques. In Kirov Park, ministers, directors, administrators, editors and even the heads of the militia are appointed or dismissed every day. And all this not only about Georgia and the Soviet Union, but about foreign countries as well.

Kirov Park is overflowing with retired people, with girls who are being ogled by Red Army soldiers, with citizens spending the summer in Tiflis, with mothers and children and old men and old women, with marriageable girls and eligible young men, with football fans and homeless students and students in general.

Each category has its own corner: the chess players sit in a quiet place, domino players near some tree stumps, the football fans near the soft-drink stands, the politicians at the lunch pavilion. Lovers are usually to be found under the shadows of the weeping willows and mulberry trees, while retired people are found under the loudspeakers hanging from a lamp post, and mothers with children go to the fountains which have no water, and so on.

What attracts so many people to Kirov Park? Kirov Park, like many other good parks, used to be a cemetery. The grave of Daniel Tchonkadze is here. What else? There is a mountain climbers' club, a basketball court, a cinema, a monument to Kirov. I personally like Kirov Park because it is near my house and near the Vera market.

It is almost dusk. I am sitting on a long bench under a fir tree and I am watching the people walking by. Last year this couple looked much better than now. How worn out they seem! They move so slowly that it takes them an hour to walk from the park entrance to my bench. Next year they probably won't come here at all. The time will come when I, too, will move in the same way. And then cease to exist.

Kirov Park used to be a cemetery. The Vera cemetery is closed now, and no one is buried there anymore. Probably it will be turned into a park in a year or two. The Vake cemetery is full to overflowing, so it will soon have to be closed.

After the Vera becomes a park, and people begin to stroll there, my friends will say: "This used to be a cemetery." By the time I'm dead the Vake cemetery will probably be a park, and so on to infinity—all cemeteries will be turned into parks, pretty parks. It makes me laugh.

When they closed the Vera cemetery and opened the new one at Vake, it was almost a desert. There was no grass, nothing grew there. But then someone planted a willow at the head of a grave, someone else planted a mulberry tree, then a fir, a plane tree, a pine, and so on. People brought water there from far away, from pools, from the Vera River. They brought it on the backs of donkeys, and on their own backs, in barrels, jars, even in their hands. They sold their possessions, just to have money to care for the trees. And the trees grew and grew; they shaded the graves, cooled the air, rustled and rustled. They made the cemetery beautiful and in their shade everyone who came there relaxed and blossomed as the trees themselves blossomed.

It will be beautiful, this park made from the Vake cemetery. When you think about it, it seems that life, in the end, is nothing but an infinite process of turning cemeteries into parks. Nothing more. By God, it is ridiculous!

"How are you, Teymo?"

"How are you doing, Karthlos!"

"Did you go to the football game?"

"No." Karthlos sat down beside me.

"Why not?"

"I don't like football," I replied.

"What do you like?" Karthlos smiled.

"Grape candy," I said, smiling.

"Take some with you to the stadium and eat it there," Karthlos suggested.

"From now on I will," I promised.

"If you could have seen Basa play today, you would have gone wild," Karthlos said.

"What did he do that was so extraordinary?"

"Marhania tossed the ball to Khotcho, Khotcho

made a long pass to Afto, Afto dribbled away and
two players who were guarding Basa suddenly took
off toward Afto . . ."

"What did Basa do?" I interrupted. Karthlos
looked at me with disdain.

"It's no use talking to you, stupid!" he said and
shook his head.

"Who won?"

"We were out of luck. We're head and shoulders
better than they are, but they won, four to one."

"I can see that we played a good game!"

"You can see nothing of the sort, and it's no use
talking to you about it. Basa is a born coach, a real
leader, another Stravinsky," Karthlos exclaimed rap-
turously, looking at the other students, who were
joining us.

"You found just the right person to talk to," Elgudja said to Karthlos, pushing me aside and sitting
down between us. The boys began to laugh.

"Whoever called football a mere sport should be
damned," Karthlos said.

"What is football if it is not a sport?" I asked.

"It is a real art!" Goguia replied.

"Then who is Beethoven?" I asked.

"In his own specialty Basa is Beethoven, and
Caruso, too!"

"In what way?"

"In sport, of course!" Goguia said, thrusting his
face close to mine.

"You mean then that football is a sport," I said,
catching him out in his illogical reason.

"Sport is writing poems like yours!" Karthlos interrupted. His listeners were pleased and applauded
him. If I had any confidence in my poems, I would
have continued the discussion, but since I had no
confidence in them I preferred to remain silent.

"Have you finished?" Elgudja asked me.

"I have finished," I said, and covered my mouth
with my hand.

"It's decided then that football is an art!" Goguia concluded, hitting me on the shoulder.

"Yes, of course: Basa is Beethoven, Afto is Mozart, Gagnidze is Cervantes, Khocholava is Tolstoi, Marhania is Mark Twain, and Kaloev is Pushkin. Of course . . ."

"Please don't leave out Michelangelo!" Nodar Dvalia said. His nickname was Gapon. We all laughed.

"Gapon, you have probably got some news!" Goguia Demetradze addressed him.

"Yesterday the Voice of America broadcast that a secretion from Spanish ants makes hair grow." Gapon had not let us down.

"Dammit, that's our luck! Even our ants are no use to us!" Goguia patted his bald head.

"What's going on?" asked Karlo, who had just arrived. A little boy, with large eyes and a big nose and freckles, accompanied him.

"How are you, Karlo?" I asked. "Whose little boy is this?"

"My nephew."

"What's your name, boy?"

"Guia."

"Bravo!"

"Do you know any poems?"

"Yes."

"Say one for us."

"I don't want to," the little boy said, and tugged at his uncle's sleeve.

"Sit down!" his uncle said, cuffing him on the head. The boy sat down.

"I took him to the doctor today," Karlo said.

"Is he sick?" I asked.

"Sick? He is as strong as a horse!"

"Then, why go to the doctor?"

"He drives us out of our minds! He is a prodigy. He multiplies, divides, adds and subtracts any number."

"That's impossible," said Gapon, surprised.

"Guia, what's three times three?" his uncle asked.

"Nine," the child answered in a flash.

"Bravo!" we exclaimed, surprised.

"Eleven minus two?"

"Nine!"

"Five plus four?"

"Nine!"

"One thousand seven hundred and twelve minus one thousand seven hundred and three?"

"Nine!"

"Amazing!" we all exclaimed. The child stood there as though sent by God. All he lacked was a halo.

"Two thousand minus one thousand nine hundred and ninety-one?"

"Nine!" the boy repeated.

"Now, I'll ask one," Gapon said.

"He won't answer anyone else," his uncle replied, trying to avoid any interference.

"I only want to ask one question—that's all," Gapon insisted.

"Go out and play, boy," his uncle said, pushing him.

"Don't hit him on the head, you might injure it," Karthlos warned.

"Two plus four is how many, boy?" Gapon said, not giving him time to escape.

"Nine!" the boy answered without blinking. The boys began to yell with laughter.

I fell off the bench from laughing so hard.

"So that's it!" Gapon said.

"He really needs a doctor's help!" Karthlos said.

"How old are you, child?" I asked, when I could breathe again.

"Nine!" the child said, and ran away.

"I've never seen a nephew so much like his uncle!" Elgudja said, choking.

"Well, stupid, were you able to count to nine when you were his age?" Karlo asked angrily.

"But what did the doctor tell you?"

"Take care of him!"

"Look after him before it's too late," Goguia Demetradze urged.

"Why are you making fun of me?" Karlo said.

"I can't help it. I don't really care, but Muskhelishvili had better watch out, because if this child continues he will put him out of business in two years," Goguia said. The boys broke down laughing. Karlo looked at us for a moment and then turned and went outside where the boy was playing.

"Follow him, Teymo, or he'll beat him up!" Karthlos said.

I got up. I went out to the pavilion. Karlo and his nephew, the new Einstein, were nowhere to be seen. I stopped by a bench where two old men were playing chess. I looked at the board. The bald man, playing the white, had been checkmated in three moves. The old man with reddish hair, who was playing the black, leaned his head on his hands and waited, his eyes squinting. It was white's turn, but he seemed not to realize it.

"Are you angry with me?" asked the man with reddish hair.

"What's the matter?" the bald man asked in astonishment.

"Play."

"Is it my turn?"

"Whose else could it be?"

"Why didn't you say so?"

"Saying does nothing. The important thing is to play."

"Well, without a queen, 'it is impossible to catch our Arsena,' "[1] hummed white, and he moved a pawn forward.

---

[1] Arsena Odselashvili is a bandit folk hero like Robin Hood.

"Check!" he said. "I am Arsena!" The black continued humming.

"I haven't yet removed my hand!" white said, returning his piece to the same place.

"Please play," black said. White played the knight.

"The knight can't move that way!" black said, correcting the move.

"Then I will play it this way," said white, and again he moved the pawn.

"Check!"

"It was not my move, it was yours!" white said.

"All right." Black did not protest.

"Play!"

"Check!"

"Move the king, and he won't be able to check you," I suggested.

"Get out of our way! It's none of your business!" the red-headed old man said, bringing me to myself.

As a matter of fact, it wasn't my business at all. But I didn't go away. I sat down. The old men began another game. While they were making their first moves, I watched the people. A young girl was sitting with her back toward me. She crossed her legs and leaned against the bench with her right arm, holding a book in her left hand so that the light fell on it. She was reading something very diligently. Her sunburnt legs were very pretty. She was wearing a short skirt and her knees were visible. Her black hair fell across her cheek, and it was impossible to see her face.

"There, the game is finished!"

"I haven't conceded yet!"

"I say it's already finished!" the old man began to shout loudly.

The girl turned toward us and I nearly fainted. It was Lia. When the old men lowered their voices, she turned away again. After a moment, she turned back and looked at me for a few seconds, and then bowed her head. She was probably wondering where she had seen me. She glanced at me surreptitiously, then turned away and continued reading.

My God, she doesn't recognize me. But then, why did she stare at me? And if she did recognize me, why does she go on reading? Did she recognize me? No, she didn't. She was reading as she had before, her back turned to me, her hair hiding her face. She read for a long time. I heard my heart beating. When I calmed down, I would speak to her. Now. I tried to stand up. My heart began to beat even more loudly. I couldn't take my eyes off Lia. Lia, Batum, the Intourist café, the shortcut, Gulika, Lia, Lia, Gulika . . . everything was mixed up. I couldn't take my eyes away. Lia was now reading in Kirov Park. She probably did not recognize me. And suddenly, I understood that she was not reading, that she recognized me. No, she wasn't reading, because I was staring at her, and she never turned a page. I must go to her, I must, I must. I went over to her.

"How are you, Lia?" I said, sitting down beside her on the bench so that I could see her face. She raised her head and pushed back her hair.

"Excuse me," she began, and she was about to say that she did not know me. "I am Teymuri," I said, interrupting her. "Teymuri. Don't you remember—in Batum the year before last."

"I do," Lia said, closing her book.

"I am Teymuri. I don't know what to say to make you remember me. Do you remember, I am the man who came to your room at night and . . ."

"I remember," Lia said, and she opened the book again.

"How are you, Lia?" I asked, to keep her from reading.

"Not too bad, thank you."

"It's amazing. When I returned from Batum I looked everywhere for you, everywhere. I was always looking for you."

"Really?" Lia said, and she smiled as one smiles when one hears a lie.

"I swear by my mother, I looked for you everywhere, and couldn't find you."

"You probably didn't look very hard," Lia said, closing the book.

"I looked very hard, I swear by my mother, and yet I couldn't find you. Today, when I was not looking for you, I found you."

"And then what?" Lia asked.

"I was very happy, that's all."

"Very pleasant."

"Did you look for me, Lia?" I asked.

"No."

"Why not?"

"Because I never lost you."

"And I was looking for you."

"What do you want from me, Teymuri?" Lia asked suddenly, standing up.

I had not expected such a question, and my tongue was silent.

"Nothing, nothing. It is nice to meet an old acquaintance."

"I was pleased too. Thank you for your attention. Good-bye," Lia said, and she made as if to go.

"Lia, if you leave me now, I'll go crazy!" I said with so much feeling that her eyes widened with surprise.

"Lia, I beg you to stay a little more, if you can."

"It's too late," Lia said, but I noticed that she hesitated.

"Just a little, just a little."

Lia sat down, and I sat down too. A long time, long in silence, went by. I sat in front of Lia, looking at her cheeks, at her dark hair falling over her face, her lips, her long curved eyelashes, her thin and wonderfully transparent fingers lying on her book, her full breasts. I heard her breathing and was overcome with a desire to embrace this beautiful woman, as a

man dying from thirst in the desert is overcome with
the desire to lie down and drink until he drowns.

I got up. Lia got up, too. Her eyes met mine.

"Let's go!" I said, in order not to say something
stupid.

Lia walked along silently. I followed beside her.
We left Kirov Park. Near the Vera market we crossed
Lenin Street and started up Belinsky Street.

"Lia, if I may go with you," I said, to break the
silence. She smiled and continued on her way.

"I probably caused you a lot of trouble that time!"
I said.

"When?"

"When I spoke about that boy with the short
hair."

"About Afto?"

"I don't know his name."

"Who was the girl who was with you?" Lia asked
suddenly.

"That girl? A friend from the university."

"But she said you were married!"

"She was probably joking. I don't remember anything like that. Did she really say that?"

"Don't you remember?"

"No!"

Lia said nothing more.

"I probably caused you a great deal of trouble,"
I began again.

"No . . . I . . ."

"Gulika isn't my wife, and never was!" But immediately I was ashamed of justifying myself.

"She was a good girl," Lia said.

"What are you reading?" I asked, to change the
subject.

Lia held the book out to me. *Alone Among the
Cannibals*, I read. "I know this book," I said. "It is
a book my mother read aloud to me when I was small.
I remember it like a dream. I asked if anyone needed
a mate on a ship going to New Zealand, where my

Eshu is waiting for me.' I think the story ended like that." Lia took the book from me and opened it at the last page.

"Where my Eshu is waiting for me," she read. "Yes, it ends like that," she said, smiling.

"And the leader is called Emai?"

"Emai." Lia nodded her head in confirmation.

"All the books my mother read to me during my childhood are still fixed in my mind. I wish my lectures would stay with me like that."

Lia laughed. We walked by the Georgian bakery, and such a fragrance struck me that I almost fainted from hunger.

"What a wonderful smell," Lia exclaimed.

"Wait a minute, Lia," I said and went into the courtyard of the bakery. The doors were closed, and I knocked. No one answered. I knocked again. The door opened slightly and someone poked his head out.

"I want some bread," I said.

"There is no bread!" he said, and closed the door in my face. I knocked again. Once again the door opened.

"I told you already, there is no bread. I can do nothing for you."

"Only one loaf, a hungry man is waiting on the street," I said.

"The sky and the earth are hungry too. If I give you bread, will you support my family later on?" he asked me.

"Don't say no. Please, give me a loaf."

"Have you five rubles?" he asked me.

"I have three."

"We don't bake for three rubles."

"Pick out a small loaf for me."

"What a bore you are." The baker was taken aback. He closed the door, but a moment later, it opened again and a round, warm loaf was thrust out to me.

"Take it and go."

I gave him three rubles and took the bread.

"Thank you, sir."

"Think nothing of it."

I went back to the street. Under the acacia tree where I had left Lia, there was no one. I looked all around, but the street was empty. "Lia!" I called. Someone turned and looked back, but it was not Lia. Something broke in my heart, and my heart burned, as though someone had poured boiling water into it. She had gone away . . . and how would I ever find her again? If only I knew why she had gone!

She had probably not been pleased at meeting me again. Had I said anything I shouldn't have? She probably hadn't wanted to be seen with me. She probably didn't want me. Once more, my heart began to burn. I sat down on the curb, the warm loaf of Georgian bread pressed to my heart.

O God, to go to so much trouble, to find her at last, and to lose her so stupidly!

What did you lose, and when did you look? a voice said.

For two long years I looked for her.

Not for one day did you look.

Then why was I so happy to see her again?

I don't know why you were happy. Anyone would be happy to see her.

Probably, but no one could be happy as I was happy. How could I have lost her so stupidly?

You will find her again, if you really want to.

Where? Where can I find her?

The bread warmed my heart and something within me melted and spilled into my veins with a pleasant sensation. I broke off a corner of the crust and began to eat it.

How stupid of me to lose her, idiot that I am! Where can I find her, and when?

I stood up and started down Lenin Street. What did I want this damned bread for? I only knew . . . I arrived at the Vera market. On the corner of Melik-

hishvili and Lenin Streets, several people were waiting
for the tram. I was too lazy to walk and so I too
waited for the tram. Two men were waiting for the
bus, with a thirty-year-old, rather plump woman, pretty
and blond. She was carrying a heavy handbag, and
wearing a cheap dress with a worn collar and sleeves.
Her eyebrows were heavily plucked, her eyelashes
were stiff with mascara, her face heavily made-up.
Although she was pretty, she was slightly common.
I stood beside her, and she looked at me as though
I were some kind of hoodlum. I felt uneasy and
glanced away. Only then did I realize that I was
still holding the bread clutched to my chest, chew-
ing on the end. I hastily swallowed what I had in my
mouth, tucked the bread under my arm and looked
at the woman. She couldn't help laughing, and turned
away. I laughed too.

"Does it taste good?" she asked me.

"Wonderful! Would you like some?" I tore off a
crust of bread.

"No, thank you."

"Do you live far away?" I asked.

"Not very far."

"I live near, too."

"I've been waiting an hour for the tram, and nothing has come along. I could have been home hours
ago," the woman said.

"What if we walk?" I said, boldly.

"If I didn't have this heavy bag," the woman said,
looking sad and frowning.

"I'll carry it for you!"

"But I can't let you go to that trouble!"

"It's nothing, really. Give it to me."

"No, I can't take advantage of your generosity!"
And we each tried to hold the bag. In the end I won
out and took the bag, which wasn't so heavy after
all.

We entered a tiny courtyard through an iron gate
at the end of Union Street. In the middle of the

courtyard a fountain dripped and gurgled. Overhead, snow-white linen and sheets hung from ropes crisscrossed in every direction. The woman took a key and went up to a white-curtained, iron-bound door which opened directly onto the courtyard. The door opened, the woman entered and turned on a light.

"Come in!" she said.

I entered and set her bag down near an oil stove on the glass-enclosed porch.

"Sit down," she said, and arranged the cushions on the sofa.

I sat. The room was small, perhaps fifteen or sixteen square meters. There was a rug-covered couch, on which I was sitting, a bed covered with a green blanket, one round table, four chairs, a bookcase and a wardrobe with a mirrored door. That was all. The woman opened the wardrobe, took out a rose-patterned dressing gown and then, standing in front of the mirror, she began to take off her dress and underwear, completely without modesty. She was plump and strong, with a white-marble body, round shoulders and high breasts. I stopped breathing. I looked away. She put the dressing gown on and sat down at the table.

"Shall we eat something?" she said.

I put the bread, which I was still holding in my hand, on the table. The woman got up, went to the cupboard and brought out some cheese, anchovy paste and half a bottle of vodka.

"Come," she said.

I stood up and then sat down at the table. The woman poured the vodka.

"To our healths!" she said. "I thank you for accompanying me. My name is Lida. And yours . . . ?" she asked, and touched her glass to mine.

"My name is Teymuri. Your health!"

"And to our friendship."

"Long life!"

We drank.

"This is my husband—he was killed in the war," she said, looking at a picture hanging on the wall. A young, beardless man smiled at us.

"I took him for your son!" I said.

"My husband! How old are you?"

"Twenty-two."

"He was twenty-three," Lida said. She poured another drink for herself and one for me.

"I must go," I said, and stood up.

"Oh, wait. We have to finish the bottle," she said. I sat down.

"To our future!"

"To our future!"

We drank a third glass.

"Our future!"

"Lida, may I sit beside you?" I said, and the room swayed and my forehead began to burn.

"Please," Lida said, smiling and closing her eyes.

I sat beside her and put my hands on her lap. Lida said nothing. She neither opened her eyes nor stopped smiling; she just rubbed her temples with both hands and remained like that. I put my arm around her shoulder, pulled her to me and kissed her, first under the ear, then on the neck and lips. Even today I remember the smell of her, an unknown, an unexplained, unheard, wonderful smell of the earth, of the sun, of wheat, of blood, of sweat, of the sea, of everything—everything that is called happiness . . . life, everything in the world.

"Lida, darling, I want to stay with you . . . if it's possible . . . Lida," I was whispering and pressing her to me.

Lida said nothing.

"Lida, I want to stay, my dear Lida, my adored Lida—"

Lida turned to me, looked at me for a long time with her large eyes and then she suddenly stood up. I stood up too.

"Stay with me!" she said, and the room began to

sway again, then to turn, turn . . . everything turned upside down. When I came to, after a while, it was dark in the room. Lida was in bed, looking at me.

"Come here," she said. I did not move.

"Come to me," Lida repeated, her voice echoing from somewhere, from a fairy story.

"Come, come, come!" the voice from a fairy story roared into my temples and ears, and I went into the story.

It was a forest dense with pine trees, birches, oaks, firs and willows—stretching toward heaven, reaching the sun . . . a forest swimming in a gold and emerald sea. I stood barefoot in the middle of the forest, my soles pricked by the pine needles. With raised hands, I looked up at the fading sunbeams among the leaves, and I spoke to God:

"O God on high!"

I breathed the sky, I bathed in the sunbeams, I was rooted in the earth and twice as tall as the forest—high, powerful and happy.

"O God on high! I thank thee, God!"

Then the sunbeams suddenly changed to fire, the flame blazed and fire enveloped the sky and the forest. The fire embraced and consumed the air, consumed the air. O God! Help me! I am burning! I stood, and I was burning like the pine standing before me and the pine needles under my feet. O God, help me! Help me! Then I was tearing out the huge oaks and beeches, the birches and the pines, by the roots; I was breaking them across my knees, I smashed and tore everything around me and flung it to the ground and called on God, but there was no sign of Him, and I fell sobbing to the earth. But God listened to my prayers. Rain fell—remarkably warm and caressing rain. It grew and grew. The fire was put out, and air—hot, sweet, white as milk, reigned everywhere. I clung to the wet earth as to my life and the earth pressed itself upon me and we wept together—the sky, the earth and I, and the earth like a live thing, was whispering to me:

"Teymuri, my joy. Teymuri, my sun, my life."

"Teymo, Teymuri, get up and go now. Go, Teymuri, dawn is coming up. Go, so the neighbors won't see you." Lida awakened me.

I got up at once and put on my clothes.

"Aren't you getting up, too?" I said.

"No, I'm on the night shift today," Lida said.

"On the night shift? Where do you work?" I asked.

"In the silk factory."

"What do you do there?"

"I make sauerkraut," Lida laughed.

"Lida, may I come to you again?" I said, and sat down on the edge of the bed.

"If you miss me. Otherwise, I don't advise it. It's not worthwhile. Think of it as a dream."

"I shall miss you," I said sincerely. Lida laughed.

"We shall see. But I don't advise it. Eat the rest of your bread and go," Lida said and waved her hand toward the table.

"That bread made me lose a girl I lost for two years and found yesterday," I said, and sat down at the table. There was a little bit of vodka left in the bottle.

"What girl?" Lida was interested.

"I met Lia in Batum. I knew her for just one day. Then I didn't see her for two whole years; today I saw her in Kirov Park . . . and while I was walking with her I went off to buy this bread in the bakery on Belinsky Street. When I came out, she was gone!"

"She disappeared?" Lida laughed.

"Disappeared, vanished!" I said. "This bread ruined me!"

"Then it must be true that 'not by bread alone' . . ."

"What did you say?"

" 'And Jesus answered him saying: "It is written, that man shall not live by bread alone, but by every word of God." ' " Lida sang out the words.

"Where is this written?" I asked.

"In the Bible."

"What else is there in the Bible?" I asked idly, and poured a glass of vodka.

"What else?" Lida said, and closed her eyes. "I shall remember in a minute . . . It says: 'And I say unto you, whosoever shall put away his wife, except it be for fornication, and shall marry another, committeth adultery; and whosoever marrieth her which is put away doth commit adultery.' "

I listened to Lida with astonishment. When she opened her eyes and saw me looking so surprised, she smiled.

"Haven't you read the Gospels?"

"No," I said.

"Well, it's there on the shelf—the third book from the right, the one with a blue cover. It says *New Testament*. Read it, it might be useful."

I stood up, took the book from the shelf, and opened it.

"Read it at home. You must go now!"

"Thank you, Lida. When I've read it, I'll bring it back to you."

"Don't bring it back. I know it by heart."

I went once more to the bed, and kissed her on the cheek.

"Thank you, Lida."

"That's all right."

"You are a very nice woman, Lida, a very good woman."

"I don't know, Teymo," she shrugged.

"Good-bye."

"Good-bye."

I left the room and carefully closed the door behind me. Tiflis was swimming in a milky fog. From far off came the squeaky noise of the morning streetcars and the deep, hoarse sound of the factory sirens. The city gleamed under pale lamps. It was rubbing its eyes, stretching itself. It was like a huge flock of sheep awaking after a peaceful night on the bank of the Mtkvari River.

Why Are You
Leaving Me?

———

Mother opened the door. She was wearing a white scarf over her shoulders and she looked very pale.

"Where have you been for so long, my son? I nearly died from worrying about you."

"I was at Guram's," I lied.

"Well, why didn't you let me know, especially at a time like this?"

"What do you mean—a time like this?"

"Haven't you heard?" my mother said in a surprised voice.

"What should I have heard?"

"We are done for, my son! Stalin is paralyzed!" My mother sat down at the table, half dead.

"Mother, have you lost your mind?" I asked, trembling.

"Yes, I have, I have. The radio said that Stalin has had a hemorrhage."

"Well, then?"

"Well, they say his condition is very critical. We are done for, son!"

"What are you trying to tell me, Mother?" I said, putting on my raincoat.

"I am ill. Don't leave me now. Don't go out. I am very sick, my child, very sick." She had no color and two tears were falling down her cheeks. I wanted to know what was troubling her, what pain she was feeling, why she was crying. Probably I would never know, and even if I did, I would never be able to explain in so many words why this good, frightened, gray-haired little woman was crying, on this terrible day.

"Don't go out, son. Stay home. I am feeling very ill," my mother repeated, and she forced me to sit down.

"What's the matter with you, Mother? I will go to see Guram. I'll go to the university and find out the news, and then I'll come home. Meanwhile, calm yourself, Mother, and go to bed. I will go away, and I'll be back very soon." I kissed her, and held her in my arms. She seemed to be quieter.

"Go," she said. "But come back soon." She allowed me to leave. I went out, but she caught up with me at the door.

"Son."

"What is it, Mother?"

"Say nothing, my son!"

"Say nothing about what?"

"Don't say that Stalin has had a stroke!"

"Why, Mother, if the radio has broadcast it, probably the whole world knows about it."

"Don't mention it! If the radio says it, let it say it, but don't you speak about it, if you love your mother!" She pressed my hand to her breast.

"All right, Mother," I promised, and ran down the stairs at breakneck speed.

Students, lecturers, professors, guards, janitors, party members and non-party members, unionists, all were standing bareheaded and stock still. The empty lecture rooms, laboratories, offices, deans' offices, libraries, reading rooms, all looked as though the plague had struck, and people, frightened, had hurriedly left their homes—the villages and the cities. All day and all night, and all the next day and night, the university was like a huge hall in some vast vaulted temple, where innumerable worshippers knelt with tears in their eyes, gazing at the loudspeaker with prayers and supplications, the loudspeaker on the stage in the club room where, every two hours, the terrible news was being announced.

At midnight, I heard strange sounds. I raised my head. My mother was tossing and turning on the bed, groaning and muttering. I jumped up and ran to the bed.

"Mother, what is happening, Mother!" I felt as though I were dreaming.

"The gown, the gown!" she said, staring at me.

"What gown, Mother?"

"White gown, the white gown."

"What do you want, Mother?"

"Bring me the white gown. I am dying!"

"Mother," I shouted, shaking her.

"My head is bursting, son. Bring me the white gown!"

I dashed to the wardrobe and brought her the white gown.

"Go!" my mother ordered. I guessed that she wanted to put the gown on, and went out of the room. I ran to the neighbor's door.

"Eliko, Eliko!" I called. No one answered me.

"Eliko!" I shouted, kicking at the door. No one answered. Everyone had gone out. I ran back into the room. Mother was lying on her back, staring at the ceiling. She was breathing heavily, and tears were running down over her face.

"Mother!"

"This . . . nothing . . . help . . . the gown . . . put it on me. I can't lift my head," she said, gasping.

I helped her put on the gown.

"So, it is better . . . like the spring . . . white . . . white . . ."

"What are you saying, my mother?" She smiled.

"In a minute, it will all be over, everything . . . Do not be afraid, my son."

"Mother! Mother, do not kill me. I will run and get the doctor!" I cried.

"Don't leave me," she said, shaking her head.

"Where does it hurt, what do you want? Tell me, Mother, my darling!"

"My boy, my clever boy, I want nothing except to die in your arms."

"Don't talk like that, my mother, don't ruin my life. Mother, do you hear, do not leave me, do not ruin me. I'll kill myself!"

"I am dying, my son!"

"Are you dying now, now that I have learned to know you . . . when I have learned finally to call you mother, when I have at last found you, Mother . . . are you mad?" I was sobbing, and lay my head on her breast.

"Light the light, son," she said, and moved her hand across my face. I stood up and lit the lamp.

"Stay there!" she said. I stood by the door. My mother looked at me for a long, long time. Then she closed her eyes, and when she opened them again, I was still standing there, by the door. My mother gave me a sign with her eyes to come to her. I went, slowly. She stared insistently at me, not blinking. I drew near, knelt before her and put my hands on her cheeks. Her face was on fire.

"Mama, mama, what is wrong!" I began to cry, and my mother closed her eyes again.

"I see you, in the flesh, I see you so clearly, this is how I will remember you, this is how you will be with me always. Thank you, my God, thank you, my God, thank you . . ." She suddenly became delirious.

"The white gown . . ."

"But I have already put it on for you, my mother."

"Teymuri, Teymuri, my little boy . . ."

"Mother, do not go, do not destroy me . . . don't leave me. Mama, what would I do without you, what will I do all alone? Tell me, Mother . . ." I cried.

"How big he has grown . . . how big he is, a man, a real man . . ."

"Mother, do not drive me mad . . . do not die . . . Are you not ashamed?"

"Be well, my son . . . the sun, the sea, the whole world is yours . . ."

"Mother!"

"Who is making my little Teymuri cry, who is making him cry?" My mother took my neck between her hands and drew me to her, kissing me hard, strongly, and then more and more weakly, with less and less force. In the end she was only touching her burning lips to my cheek. She left them there, whispering into my ear:

"One minute, one second, O God, where are you, God? You are sweating, my son . . . my life is yours . . . you have run too hard, my son . . . No, don't leave, don't go into the yard, I will go, I am going, obey your grandmother until I return . . ."

"Mother, do not leave, do not go, Mother dear, open your eyes, mama, open your eyes . . . open them, please!" I cried.

My mother shook her head, as if to say no, and then her arms slipped from my neck and fell on the bed as though they had been cut down.

"Mother!!"

"Thank God. . . it is over," my mother said, and her chin began to tremble. Then two big tears fell from her eyes and she ceased to breathe.

I went out to the glassed-walled gallery and opened all the windows. The cold air burst into the room; it dried my tears and burned my cheeks like alum. A thick mist lay in the Varasi ravine. Tiflis slept, the naked acacia trees swayed slightly, plunged in the deep sleep of dawn. On Mtatsminda all was dark, but far, far in the settlement of Semionov, I could see a light. The sky was studded with stars, and that little light was like someone's total star, fallen from the enormous sky.

I stood there for a long time, and looked at that light. Why was a light burning at such an hour? Perhaps there, too, someone had just closed his eyes for the last time, for eternity. Or maybe an infant has just opened his eyes for the first time. Or is there a wedding—a big and happy wedding party?

I wanted to scream, to shout from here to that light and ask what is going on. Why was it burning at such an hour, for what and for whom? But perhaps is was not a lamp at all. Perhaps it is my mother's total star, come down from the sky to look for her. Suddenly I was afraid of my loneliness. I wanted the dawn to come, I wanted to shriek, to move the earth and sky, to scream so that the star should know that my mother and I were here. But the star flickered out.

In Tiflis day was breaking.

I went back to the room. I covered my mother with a sheet and sat at the table. The Bible I had brought home with me the day before was on the table. Idly, I turned the pages and began to read.

"And at the ninth hour Jesus cried with a loud voice, saying, Eloi, Eloi, lama sabachthani? which is, being interpreted, My God, my God, why hast thou forsaken me?"

Then a long time went by. Someone knocked at the

door and came in slowly. I looked around. Guram stood in the room.

"Stalin is dead," he whispered.

"What did you say?"

"Stalin is dead."

Lia

    "Hello, Lia."
    "How did you find me?"
"I searched for you and I found you!"
"Come in."
I entered the room and sat down in a corner.
Lia buttoned the neck of her dressing gown and sat
down in another corner.
"How are you, Lia?" I asked.
"Not too bad, thank you," she said.
"Where did you go, Lia, that night?"
"I went nowhere. I waited and waited and finally
I left," she smiled.
"And then?"
"Then nothing. I just left."

195

"And afterward. Didn't you expect me?"

"Not today."

"When, then?"

"I don't know."

"But did you expect me?"

"Yes," Lia said, and bowed her head.

I don't know why, but I wanted to cry.

"Lia, I have searched so hard for you, searched day and night."

Lia uncovered a bowl standing on the table, filled with figs and peaches.

"Please take some," she said, and sat down again, in the corner. Silence fell in the room.

"I don't know how to behave," Lia said, after the silence had stretched on for a long time.

"Neither do I," I said. To hide my uneasiness, I took out a cigarette.

"Lia, my mother died."

"I know," Lia said, and I was not astonished.

"Lia, do you have any vodka?" I asked suddenly.

Lia stood up without speaking. She took from the cupboard a crystal pitcher of rosy-looking vodka and put it before me. I filled a glass. I wanted to say something, but I couldn't, and so I drank in silence. Lia didn't take her eyes off me. I drank a second glass in the same way, and only after a third did I speak.

"Lia, you don't know me. You probably don't even know who I am. Because I'm drinking vodka, do you think I'm a drunkard? This is the first time in my life I've ever drunk vodka alone. Won't you drink a little too?"

Lia poured a vodka and drank.

"What a nice girl you are, Lia," I said, and poured another drink. "You don't know me, Lia, but I know you as well as I know my own hand." I stretched out my hand, and noticed it was trembling. "You may not believe me, I don't expect you to—but do you think I have never met you in these last two years? I have met you every day, I have spoken with you, I have listened to you. There is no place where we haven't been together. A thousand times I have told you the things I am saying now. And you don't know me at all," I said, and drank again.

"I know you, Teymo," Lia said.

"Do you know that I love you?" I said, and stood up.

"I know everything except that," Lia said, and she stood up too.

I came close to her and looked into her huge, clever eyes, and touched her cheek with a trembling hand.

"No, no. Don't come too close to me, Teymuri, I beg you," Lia said, and backed away.

"Lia, my Lia, don't you know how much I love you?"

"I know, Teymuri. But just don't come near me now. Don't come!" Lia said, pressing herself to the wall.

But I came to her. I heard the beating of her heart, and felt her quick hot breath.

"My darling Lia," I whispered.

"Teymo, go away now. Leave me alone, Teymuri. I beg you, go now! Go!" Lia's eyes were filled with tears.

"Lia, don't send me away now. It would be kinder to kill me," I implored her.

"All right. But don't touch me, Teymuri, my Teymuri! I beg you, if you love me, don't touch me."

She stood before me, like the goddess of love, like love itself, and asked me, Teymuraz Baramidze, crazy with love, not to touch her. And I did not dare go against her will. I turned around and sat down again on the chair. For a long time I sat with my head bent. Then Lia came to me and put her hand on my head. I pressed her hot hands to my cheek and closed my eyes. Lia gently took her hand away and again stroked my cheek.

"Go now, Teymuri, and come back tomorrow, the day after tomorrow, whenever you wish . . . come then," she said in a low voice.

"Lia, come with me!" I asked.

"Where?"

"Go, get dressed! We will walk in the city!"

"It's too late now. Some other day."

"No, now! If you love me, get dressed and come with me, Lia. If you don't come I will kill myself! Please!" Lia hesitated for a long time. Then she dressed and we went out.

That night Tiflis was like a precious jewel. And I was a beggar, whose every wish Tiflis the blessed fulfilled.

"Long life to you, Arthavaz!"

"Long life to you . . . who are you?"

"Teymuri."

"Which Teymuri?"

"Don't you remember me . . . how I came to you three years ago, at night?"

"Uhhh, no, I don't remember . . ."

"Teymuri, whose mother returned from exile, don't you remember?"

"You wretch . . . you forgot me."

"How are you, Uncle Arthavaz?"

"How should I be?—an old man, lost to the world, my sight growing weaker every day, growing deaf and weak in the knees?"

"Don't worry, Uncle Arthavaz, you'll be all right."

"And how are you? Who is this pretty girl?"

"I brought her to introduce her to you. This is my fiancée, Lia."

"Why couldn't you bring her in the daytime? I can hardly see at night . . . but she seems to be good-looking."

"Just look at her, Uncle Arthavaz. She's beautiful!"

"Yes, yes . . . a pretty face is all very well, but it's what's inside that counts!"

"She is good, too."

"Well, God bless you."

"Thank you, Uncle Arthavaz."

"How is your mother?"

"She's gone."

"May God console you."

"Thank you."

"It is hard to lose one's mother."

"It is very hard, Uncle Arthavaz."

"You have brought me sad news!"

"Yes, it couldn't be helped. Good-bye, Uncle Artha-vaz."

"Don't forget me, boy. Come to see me again, and bring me good news."

"I will, Uncle Arthavaz."

"Do you have any cigarettes?"

"Sure, I have cigarettes! Here, and take some matches."

"Thank you."

"Be well!"

"Be happy!

"Guram! Guuurraam!"

"Are you out of your mind, yelling like that in the middle of the night?"

"Come down here, I have got something to show you!"

"Tomorrow. I'm in bed."

"Come down! It's all the same to me . . . I won't let you sleep!"

"Uuuh . . . get on with you!"

"Come down! I want you to meet Lia."

"Oh!"

"How are you, Guram?"

"How do you do, Lia?"

"Thank you, so-so . . . and you?"

"I will probably go out of my mind. Where have you come from?"

"From the house."

"Oh."

"And where are you going?"

"Home."

"I will really go out of my mind."

"Go back to bed."

"How do you expect me to sleep now?"

"Well, stay there and stare! Good-bye."

"Wait, wait. Do you . . ."

"Yes, Lia and I love each other!"

"Really, Lia?"

"Yes."

"Good night."

"Will we see you tomorrow?"

"Yes! Both of you?"

"From now on, it's always both of us!"

"I swear I'm going out of my mind!"

"We're leaving."

I have come. It is I, your flesh and blood, standing beside your tombstone. I am your child. I stand by your tombstone and I am not shy, because I want you to feel my presence. I weep at your grave and I am not ashamed to do so in front of Lia, in front of you. I want Lia to know what you were for me. I want her to protect and mourn over this grave just as I do, because from this day on, she and I are one.

I am your child. In gratitude for your great love I dug your grave with my own hands, with my own hands I lowered you into it, and placed this large stone on your breast. I am your child. I found you with great difficulty, but I found you and I will never lose you again, because this cemetery is mine.

This is Lia, a part of that life which you left to me in the world. You left me so much life that I cannot possibly use it up alone. For that reason, don't be hurt that I gave part of our life—yours and mine—to her.

I am your child. Your flesh and blood. I stand here among the graves at midnight and I am not afraid. I am not afraid because the thing I feared above all has already happened. That was your death; and because I no longer fear death, I no longer fear life.

It does not disturb me that this cemetery like many others is being turned into a park, a large and pretty park. I have planted a lime tree on your grave. I will make it grow and blossom. In the future, Lia and I will come to your grave with our children, and the tree will have grown into a vast, green, cool shade, and my children will play in your greenness, your coolness and shade. Perhaps they will carve their names on your breast, but don't be hurt: the same thing will probably happen at my grave and Lia's grave. The lime tree will blossom and grow and every one of our graves will become part of the life of this world. And every cemetery will be turned into a park, and so it will be for all eternity.

I am standing at your grave. I, happy and unhappy, innocent and guilty, strong and weak—but I am stronger than you and I know you would be happy for that.

I am at your grave at midnight. I am no preacher. Forgive me, that I cannot say anything worthy of you, my mother.

Thou Shalt Not Kill

He was stretched on his back in the hall, breathing his last. I bent and looked down into his eyes. His eyes did not focus. I picked him up on my back and carried him to the third floor. I propped him against his door, checked his pockets, found the key, opened the door and set him down on the rug-covered sofa in his workroom. I loosened his tie, took off his belt and shoes.

Abibo lay before me, and he was dying. The man who spit on my soul, destroyed me, sacrificed me, was dying, and his soul was now in my hands.

Now I will kill him—but no, he will die by himself. I will just sit and look at him until he dies. Perhaps he wants water. I am the only source of water for him now, and I want him to know that my fountain is dry; perhaps he wants to hear a human voice and my voice will be God's blessing on him. Let him realize that I am dumb. Perhaps he wants to say something and demand attention: let him know that I am deaf. Perhaps he wants light, and I am his sun: let him know that I am not there. Perhaps he needs air and I could be his life-giving air: let him know that I am a closed window.

I am Death, standing at his head, and I will kill him if he does not die a natural death. Abibo has to know this. My hands are shaking, my mouth dry, a thousand hammers are striking my temples and saying: "Kill him, kill him, kill him! You are his death and he must know it!"

"Abibo!" I said in such a changed voice that I frightened myself.

Abibo opened his eyes and stared at me without recognition.

"It is I, Abibo!" I said.

"Help me!" he begged, and closed his eyes.

Now I had to get up, move, and for an instant I could not do it. I was paralyzed. But I stood up, went to the telephone and called an ambulance.

"Water!" Abibo said, and licked his dry lips.

I went to the kitchen, filled a glass with water and brought it to him. He drank it and began to cough.

"Air, air!" he said, struggling for breath.

I opened all the windows. Fresh air penetrated the room and only then did I notice that the room smelled of naphthalene and dust.

"Help me!" he said, and fell into a delirium.

"Don't be afraid, I will help you, the doctor will come soon," I said and sat down on the couch.

"Help me!" he repeated.

There was a knock on the door. I opened it. A very fat woman and a thin man entered the room. The fat woman was breathing heavily and the thin man held a Red Cross box in his hand.

"Where is the sick man?" the fat woman asked.

"Right there," I pointed.

"What have you done for him?"

"Nothing. I gave him water and opened the windows."

"What's his blood pressure?"

"I don't know, ma'am."

"Blood pressure," the fat woman ordered.

The thin man handed her a gauge.

"Two hundred and forty," she announced.

Then she pulled down Abibo's eyelids and asked him some questions. Abibo did not respond.

"Insulin!" the fat woman said.

"Magnesium with Novocain?" the thin man asked.

"Theophyllin too," the fat woman said.

She gave Abibo an injection.

"How did it happen?" she asked me.

"I found him in the lobby, stretched out unconscious. I brought him up here and that's all I know about it."

"You found him in time. Don't be afraid—he'll survive. We save people in worse shape than he is in," she said, and looked at her assistant.

"God bless you, doctor," I said.

"You must keep a cold towel on his neck and forehead at all times. Ice is even better," the doctor advised me.

I went to the kitchen. I brought water in a deep bowl which I put on a chair beside his pillow. I soaked a towel in the water, wrung it out and put it on his head.

"Don't be afraid," the doctor calmed me. "Are you his son?"

"No."

"Are you a brother?"

"No, ma'am. I'm only his neighbor."

"Now all he needs is quiet, nothing more. We have done everything necessary. Change the towel as often as possible. We shall be back in the morning to look at him. Now be brave," the woman doctor said.

She checked his pulse before going and nodded her head in satisfaction.

"Don't be afraid. Here, I'm leaving some cardamom with caffeine, but I don't think he'll need it," the doctor said soothingly, and they left.

I closed the door and sat down near Abibo's head. Abibo looked better already. He turned toward me and looked at me for a long time.

"Who are you?" he asked timidly.

"Teymuri."

"What happened? What's wrong with me?"

"Nothing. Go to sleep. You felt a bit ill for a while, but now you're all right."

Abibo closed his eyes, but he did not sleep. He seemed to be trying to remember something.

"Teymuri, is it you?" he asked.

"It's me, Uncle Abibo," I said, and changed his towel.

"Will I die?"

"No, the doctor says you won't die."

"What about you?"

"Don't worry. You won't die. Just go to sleep!"

"Don't leave me, boy!"

"No, don't be afraid. Go to sleep now."

Abibo looked me straight in the eyes. I suppose he believed and trusted me, for he closed his eyes and turned over on his other side.

I sat beside Abibo, changing the towel, until six in the morning. He had a very troubled sleep. Once in a while he would awaken, look at me with frightened eyes, then once more he would go into a delirious sleep. At first I was full of hatred, but to my surprise, it drained away, little by little. My head calmed down, my temples stopped throbbing. I sat beside Abibo's pillow and I looked at this man, frightened of death, diminished, broken. I sat there, empty of hatred, bearing no ill will toward him.

In front of me lay nothing—a stone, a tree, a stump—I didn't know. It was simply an object for which I felt nothing. I only looked at it and saw it. Then, something extraordinary happened. I felt pity for him, because he was a sick man, because he was my close neighbor. I was surprised to discover that I wanted to cry. I put my hand on his forehead, and rearranged the pillow. Suddenly my throat filled with compassion and pity for this man—such great pity that I could not bear to look at him any longer. I stood up. Abibo, as if he felt movement, began to rage in delirium.

"Teymuri! Teymuri!"

"I'm here."

"Don't leave me, boy! Kill me, but don't leave me!" He turned toward me.

"I won't leave you. Don't be afraid!"

"Forgive me, boy, if you can."

I put a fresh towel on his head. As I was doing so, Abibo caught my hand and began to kiss it.

"What are you doing, Uncle Abibo!" I exclaimed, and snatched my hand away.

"Forgive me, boy. Forgive me!"

I could not speak.

"Then kill me! Why don't you kill me!"

"I am no murderer, Uncle Abibo."

Abibo stared at me with his blue transparent eyes, in which I saw a tear for the first time. Abibo was crying!

The doctor came in the morning. Abibo fell asleep again and I went home. I felt a strange weakness, or lightness. I had left something big and heavy—insupportably big and heavy—in Abibo's room yesterday. To replace that, something clear, transparent, light and warm came to fill my whole body. I was drunk with relief and joy.

I leaned on the balustrade as I went up the stairs to my floor. The door of my room was open as usual. I went in—and nearly screamed. Thavera, all smiles, stood in the middle of the room!

"Ramaz! Is it you?"

"It's me, Teymo!"

"Did you run away again?"

"No! I've been pardoned!"

Then I remembered the Rector's office, the Rector holding a red pencil, his head bent over a piece of paper. I remembered the drawing he had made, of a lopeared, sad-eyed, naive red donkey. Under it the same red pencil had written *"Ramaz Korsaveli (Thavera)"* and the mysterious numbers "233." I remembered all that. I couldn't stand any more. Something broke inside me, and I began to cry.

May came to Tiflis not with gentle showers, but with downpours, lightning and thunder. Today it rained three times and after each rain the sun came out.

I opened the window and the white branch of the acacia tree darted into the room. It swayed awhile, and then remained motionless against my face, like the white hand of a beautiful woman. With reverence, I took the white acacia hand and kissed it gently. The white acacia entered my room, bringing with it countless smells of the earth, the air, the rain, the sun. This white acacia was the first to come to me and congratulate me on my birthday—May 14th. It has grown along with me in this courtyard, it is just my own age, so, naturally, it is happy about my birthday.

Not very many people will come to me today. Guram will come. He will bring a bottle of wine and drink it himself. Lia will come to my birthday party for the first time. She will come, she will sit down in the corner, she will look at me. But I don't know what she will do afterward. Will she leave, or will she stay? Perhaps she won't leave me. Perhaps if I ask her, she will stay. But the acacia, my acacia, can go nowhere, even if it wants to.

Maybe no one will come, no one will remember my birthday! If so, I shall make the rounds on foot and I will invite everybody.

"Lia, how are you? Today is my birthday. Will you come? Please?"

"Guram, don't forget. Today is my birthday! Today!"

"Excuse me, sir. It is true that you don't know me, but I know you. I see you in the street almost every day. If it's no trouble to you, please come to my house today—it's my birthday. I am twenty-four years old. Please don't stand on ceremony, I live in the neighborhood, at that house over there, fourth floor to the left. The door will be open."

"Forgive me, madam. Please don't think I am being rude, stopping an unknown lady in the street, but I would be very honored if you would come to my birthday party today. If you don't mind, it would make me very happy. You are so much like my mother."

"Uncle Arthavaz! Don't be afraid. Nobody will run away with your store of food. I won't keep you long, we'll drink just one glass—drink a toast to this night, this night that waits for daybreak."

"Thavera! Do you need to be invited? Come up and we'll celebrate my birthday together. You could even move in with me. Pack your bag and coat and come to live with me. Come up, do you hear? Don't fail me! Be sure to come! We'll have such a birthday celebration as no one has ever seen before! Come, if you love me."

"Tiflis, my Tiflis! Gather all your streets and come to my birthday party today. It doesn't matter how long you stay—come just for an hour. Am I not your child? Didn't I learn to walk in your streets and parks? Well then, come and give me your blessing, dear Tiflis."

And I know that everyone will come—everyone! In spite of the smallness of my room, there will be enough room; or if it is too small, they can come in turns to congratulate me. There is nothing extraordinary about that. What should they say to me, to congratulate me and toast my health? Nothing at all— nothing but a few words.

Your health, Teymuri! Be victorious! Be happy! Long live your friends, may you never lose faith in them! May your life be successful and your thoughts and your dreams! Long live your native country! God bless your native country and your family too! Be victorious, Teymuri!

I do not want anything more.

About the Author

Nodar Dumbadze is a man in his forties. Very little is known about this popular Georgian writer. No other of his works has appeared in English.

The Sunny Night, apparently autobiographical, was first published in the literary monthly magazine *Mnathobi* (*The Lightbringer*) in January and February of 1966. It is edited by one of Georgia's leading poets and novelists, Gregor Abashidze, and like its Russian counterpart, *Novy Mir*, is noted for its liberalism.

Dumbadze has written two other novels—*I See the Sun* and *I, Iliko, Ilarion and the Grandmother*—both of which have been made into films. He has also written poetry and film scenarios.

About the Translator

Prince George Nakashidse was born in Georgia. He is a graduate of Tbilisi State University, studied law in Heidelberg University, and holds doctorates in law and philosophy from universities in Prague. He was an assistant professor at Warsaw University and Lecturer in the Language, Literature, and History of the Caucasus at Columbia University. In the spring of 1968, he was awarded a Chapel Hill fellowship for his projected history of Georgian literature. He is presently at work on an anthology of Georgian poetry for Washington Square Press.